Written and illustrated by

THE ULTIMATE GUIDE TO
THE BIGGEST GAME

First published in Great Britain in 2014 by Osprey Publishing,
PO Box 883, Oxford, OX1 9PL, UK
PO Box 3985, New York, NY 10185-3985, USA
E-mail: info@ospreypublishing.com

Osprey Publishing is part of the Osprey Group

A CIP catalogue record for this book is available from the British Library

Print ISBN: 978 1 8472 1282 7
PDF e-book ISBN: 978 1 4728 1283 4
EPUB e-book ISBN: 978 1 4728 1284 1
Page layout by: Myriam Bell Design, UK
Typeset in Georgia, Kenyan Coffee and XXII Black Block
Originated by PDQ Media, Bungay, UK
Printed in China through World Print Ltd

15 16 17 18 19 10 9 8 7 6 5 4 3 2 1

www.ospreypublishing.com

Osprey Publishing is supporting the Woodland Trust, the UK's leading woodland conservation charity, by funding the dedication of trees.

CONTENTS

INTRODUCTION

CONGRATULATIONS!

Your application for a Mesozoic Hunting Licence has been accepted!

SO, WHAT HAPPENS NOW?

You have successfully passed your preliminary physical and psychological profile; your financial status has been approved; and your non-refundable deposit has been paid.

We will now offer you a selection of time zones in which to hunt. However, before you rush off to hunt *T-rexes* in the Maastrichtian, please read this guide. It will help inform your decision. You will then be asked to make three choices in descending order of preference. We cannot guarantee that your first preference will be the one offered. The final choice is legally binding; no discussion will be entered into.

Once you have agreed to the selection, your training and acclimatization will begin. Hunting in the Mesozoic is as much about survival as it is about the tracking and killing of your target. As such, you will be given intensive training in some of the planet's harshest environments; depending on your final choice of hunting ground, this could be the jungles of Vietnam and Sierra Leone; the plains of the Masai Mara; the Florida Everglades; or the Saharan desert. Should you choose a high carbon-dioxide environment such as the Chinle of the Upper Triassic, you will also spend time acclimatizing in high-altitude, low-oxygen locations and in specially designed tanks.

You will also be subject to intensive physical training by our highly skilled fitness teams, and to extensive and rigorous psychological profiling. The former is key to your survival in case of emergency and the latter is to provide continued assessment of your mental suitability to the stress and trauma you will face on your excursion.

These two aspects of your personal wellbeing are vital. While you may be well armed, well trained and logistically well cared for, it is worth pointing out the following maxim:

HUNTING IN THE MESOZOIC IS EXTREMELY DANGEROUS!!!

No matter how prepared you think you are, nothing can prepare you for what you are about to face. You may be an experienced hunter; you may have hunted Big Game all over the world, but this is not controlled lion hunting in South Africa. There is no room for morbidly obese braggarts squatting in an SUV with a high-powered rifle; this is not the place for supermodels overcoming food disorders by killing for sport. This is ONLY for true hunters willing to place their lives on the line and place themselves in harm's way. For many, it is a way to experience a more primal state, to imagine how our ancestors lived and died as hunter-gatherers.

But imagining that and doing it are two extremely different things. The psychological screening is to assess how you, the hunter, will cope with separation anxiety. The screening modelled on that given to astronauts, sent millions of miles from Earth without hope of being rescued.

Whilst there will be rescue available to you, many find the anxiety of being millions of years from home unendurable; many hunters have experienced breakdowns. Others, suffering from dissociative amnesia, have wandered off and been lost. You may think you have the machismo to handle such fears but bear in mind, should you allow bravado to subsume common sense, we still get paid, no matter what happens to you.

Please consider, then, carefully, your options.

IF I PASS THE TRAINING/ ACCLIMATIZATION?

Once you have been deemed fit by our staff, you will continue with exercises in both simulated and actual environments, and begin the process of familiarizing yourself with your equipment and with the logistical support who will be operating alongside you.

Your final payment covers the following field kit. Please be aware you will be expected to only use equipment sanctioned by Mesozoic Hunter Corporation (MHC)®:

- Hunting rifle (see below)
- Shotgun (see below)
- Smoke grenades: for position marking and, in emergencies, to obfuscate the hunting team from aggressive animals
- Pepper spray: a useful deterrent to any overly inquisitive or aggressive animals
- Ghillie suit: an air-conditioned camouflage suit; these are specifically adapted to each hunting zone

- Body armour: there are Kevlar composite armour plates to cover all regions of the body; experienced hunters can find these an encumbrance and choose to wear only those they consider vital. This varies from hunter to hunter; it should be pointed out that while the armour may prevent penetration by even the biggest teeth, it can do little to deter bite pressure or prevent crushing. Most experienced hunters usually wear armour plates on the arms and legs, which are considered most vulnerable to attack
- Machete: generally used as a clearing tool but, in desperate situations, can be employed as a weapon
- Rebreather and CO2 scrubbers: the Mesozoic (particularly the Triassic) has higher concentrations of carbon dioxide than the present. Not only does this result in the 'greenhouse effect' of markedly raised temperatures through the Era (again, particularly during the Triassic but also the Jurassic) but it also makes breathing a troubling affair for humans. Accordingly, the rebreather is a respiratory apparatus similar to those used by SCUBA divers; however, unlike the closed system of underwater rebreathers, the Mesozoic version works in virtually the opposite way, drawing air in and over the CO2 scrubbers, which reduce the amount of carbon dioxide and make it more palatable to human lungs. The scrubbers can be changed quickly and easily in the field
- Webbing and pony rig: the pony rig is a small air bottle and respirator used as an emergency air supply; it is hung in the small of the back from the military webbing fitted out beneath the ghillie suit
- Bergen backpack
- Compass
- Waterproofs
- Walking boots

- Bush hat
- Goggles
- Gloves
- Strobes (infra-red and white light)
- Flares
- Insect hood
- Insect repellent
- First aid kit (includes broad-spectrum antibiotics, painkillers, anaesthetic, speed glue, stapler, band aids, gauze and bandages
- Head-mounted camera: these are used to film all hunts and downloaded to a hard drive at the Forward Operating Base (FOB). All material filmed on the head cameras is copyright © Mesozoic Hunting Corporation
- MREs (Meals Ready to Eat): lightweight pre-prepared meals including hot food
- Water packs and drinking tubes
- Camping equipment: includes two-person tent, portable stove, cooking utensils, portable air-conditioning unit, UV anti-insect light, motion detectors, electric lamps and sleeping bags
- Communication equipment

Important: No hunt will be undertaken without valid life insurance coverage for the hunting team.

ORGANIZATION AND FACILITIES

Whilst many of you may already be experienced hunters, the environments and conditions you will be entering will be unfamiliar, as will the animals you will be hunting.

You will be operating in pairs. Again, some of you may only be familiar with hunting alone. However, this is non-negotiable.

For the sake of expediency, we will refer to the second team member as the 'spotter'; however, the spotter's duties include providing cover for the 'shooter' or 'hunter'; their second set of eyes is there to look for trouble while the hunter is engaging the target and therefore they are equipped with a scope or binoculars. The spotter is also armed with a shotgun containing lethal rounds, to be used in case of emergencies; the hunter is similarly equipped with a back-up shotgun, but fitted with non-lethal rounds to act as a deterrent to any inquisitive or aggressive animals.

During your month in the Mesozoic, you will operate out of a Forward Operating Base (FOB), which includes living quarters; a field hospital; a drone shack; and hangars for the helicopter/tilt-rotor pair known as the Pink Team.

THE PINK TEAM

The Pink Team derives its name from the callsigns of the two aircraft that form the flight: the 'white' utility helicopter or tilt-rotor (a UH-74 Shasta or V-32 Victor respectively), and the 'red' scout/gunship (an RAH-80 Osage).

The Pink Team's primary role is the support of the hunting team, both generally and in cases of emergency. The 'white' aircraft is used in the transport and medevac role, inserting the hunting team into their location, running supplies and extracting the team. The Osage is there to provide overwatch and, in extreme cases, cover for the white aircraft. The Pink Team is kept on five-minute standby or 'alert five'; it can be airborne in five minutes should the necessity arise and the hunting team is kept within a geographical radius that allows the Pink Team to be with the hunting party within 20 minutes should an emergency situation arise. In more dangerous environments, the Pink Team will be airborne to provide top cover for the hunting team.

A pair of aircraft are kept at the FOB as replacements should one or the other be grounded due to maintenance or mechanical failure. The FOB also hosts ground crews to service the aircraft and drones.

In addition to the Pink Team is a pair of KV-32s, a version of the Victor fitted out as an airborne tanker used for in-flight refuelling. These can refuel the Pink Team in flight and extend its flying time if the situation requires it.

DRONE COVERAGE

Once the hunting team is on the ground, drones are airborne 24/7. These are equipped with cameras (low-light, heat-sensitive, UV and infra-red, as well as white light optics) and also HV flechettes. These weapons are essentially high-velocity, warhead-less composite darts that can be used to defend the hunting team in case of extreme emergency.

The drones can be used to track target animals should the hunting team so choose; this is especially useful in areas of dense forest, where heat-sensitive cameras can distinguish animals below and help steer the hunting team to their target or away from trouble. (Some hunters prefer to use the drones only for the latter, relying on their own field craft to track prey.)

RULES OF ENGAGEMENT

One of the most frequently asked questions MHC® is asked is 'will you affect the time line?' No. No matter what Ray Bradbury wrote, you will not come back to the present to find the Earth ruled by monkeys. Why not? Well, quantum physics and temporal theory are outside the remit of this guide; you'll just have to take our word for it.

That said, the hunting expeditions are rigorously controlled. The number of animals taken is strictly limited to three per expedition. This number is also restricted to only certain types or species, according to the time period you are in. The breaking of these rules will result in prosecution by MHC®, leading to heavy fines and imprisonment. There is a self-defence clause but this will be rigorously examined in a court of law.

WHAT HAPPENS WHEN I ARRIVE AT MY CHOSEN DESTINATION?

It's worth pointing out at this juncture that we cannot guarantee precisely where your expedition will arrive in the Mesozoic. The Artificial Intelligences used to calculate the opening of the windows into the Era are about as advanced as is possible at this time but they still lack the capability to calculate a precise point in time. Each window has a plus/minus factor of approximately 1–1.5 million years. This can affect the fauna to be expected. For instance, the Morrison Formation lasts 8 million years. The aim point is the lower/mid-Morrison 150 million years ago, a point in time when the most iconic members of the fauna were common, including *Allosaurus*, *Stegosaurus* and *Diplodocus*. Any later sees a faunal changeover as the Morrison became wetter, giving rise to new genres and species, and resulting in the extinction of others.

On arrival at your destination, you will begin your familiarization training. This will include navigational exercises and Theatre Indoctrination Training (TIT) flights with the Pink Team that will allow the hunting team to develop a geographical understanding of the hunting range (termed reserves). This will be followed by 'walkabouts': on-foot safaris that are not for the purposes of hunting but for acclimatization and familiarization with the equipment and procedures to be employed.

Once familiarization is complete, your hunting team will be dropped at your first campsite; you will spend five days in the field before two days back at the FOB; followed by three similar rotations until you have completed four weeks.

YOUR DESTINATION

If this is your first (and possibly only) hunt, you now have the difficulty of choosing your destination.We have five hunting zones available:

1. Chinle Formation: Late Triassic (early-mid Norian stage) of what is now South-West North America, approximately 225–210 million years ago (mya)
2. Morrison Formation: Late Jurassic (very late Kimmeridgian to early Tithonian stage) of Mid-West North America, 152–148 mya
3. Bahariya Formation: Middle Cretaceous (Cenomanian stage) of North Africa, 98–93 mya.
4. Dinosaur Park Formation: Late Cretaceous (late Campanian stage) of Western North America, 75–72 mya
5. Hell Creek Formation: Late Cretaceous (late Maastrichtian stage) of Western North America, 66–65 mya

Each section in this book represents one particular destination and includes a story, memoir or report that not only gives you, the reader, a flavour of the various time zones but also serves as a cautionary tale. Most do not end well. They are there not to frighten you but to help inform your final choice by showing you the Mesozoic at its best and worst.

THUMP GUNS AND ELEPHANT LOADS

The basic weapon offered to the MHC® hunter is the bolt-action Ruger No.3 Elephant Load. The rifle is 41in long, with a 24in barrel and weighs 10lbs (without scopes). It uses open sights but is fitted out to carry modern optical sights. The Elephant Load fires a .505 1,300-grain cartridge with a velocity of 2,500ft/s; it can also use wildcat elephant gun cartridges that retain the .505's diameter but have a longer case and modern accelerants. These rounds have a higher muzzle velocity of 2,600ft/s without necessitating a bigger weapon and barrel to increase muzzle velocity. They can also be fitted out with Nitro Express tungsten flechette rounds with very high muzzle velocities or a 700g solid metal slug for use against particularly tough targets. These are modelled on the ironically named .577 Tyrannosaur manufactured by A-Square; even more ironically they have been found to be the best available cartridge for penetrating the skull of large Theropods. The action is smooth and simple; the rifle itself also contains very few parts, making it very reliable and easy to maintain in the field.

The second rifle is the Purdy Allosaur Express. It fires a Holland & Holland .705 NE cartridge with a maximum velocity of 2,000ft/s but the rifle itself is much lighter, only 7lbs. The Express is 361/2in long with a barrel length of 22in. It generally uses open sights but can be fitted with modern scopes. Like the Ruger, the weapon is simple to operate and easy to maintain.

Both shooter and spotter will be equipped with shotguns. These are essentially for deterring overly inquisitive or aggressive animals, or for use in extreme emergency situations (for 'emergency', read 'animal attack').

The shooter is equipped with non-lethal rounds for the shotgun: CS gas, baton rounds and 'pepper' rounds. These are generally enough to dissuade even the most persistent of predators.

However, should these fail, the spotter has a lethal load-out, including solid slug penetrators – generally considered the most effective round against large, dangerous animals.

The primary shotgun used by MHC® is the Benelli M6 12-gauge semi-automatic, which has an effective range of 165ft. The Italian-made weapon is 35in long, with an 181/2in barrel. However, it does have a folding stock, which many experienced hunters prefer collapsed when moving in confined environments such as forest. Its weight is only 81/2lbs.

The M6 generally uses a ghost ring open sight but also has a Picatinny rail on the top of the barrel for scopes and flashlights. The weapon has a 7 + 1 load (seven in the magazine, one in the chamber) and has seen action in a number of wars with armies around the world, where the weapon has proved tough and versatile. It has proved similarly effective in the Mesozoic.

THE CHINLE FORMATION

Period: Late Triassic
Age: Norian stage (225–210 mya)
Present location: South-West North America, principally Arizona
Reserve size: approx 5,000 square miles (slightly smaller than the Serengeti National Park)

CONDITIONS

The Chinle is considered to be the most arduous of the Mesozoic hunting reserves. The mean temperature is also far higher than today; dry seasons are generally 40°C (104°F) or higher, while there are prevalent 'greenhouse' conditions resulting from a greater percentage of carbon dioxide in the atmosphere (seven times more than present pre-industrial levels). This is the principal reason for the physical hardships of hunting in the Triassic; it requires the constant use of rebreathers in high-temperature, high-humidity environs. As such, much of the preparatory physical training takes place in areas of low oxygen at high altitudes to prepare the body for the remote possibility of being active without breathing equipment.

The continents are arranged into the giant supercontinent of Pangaea; the Chinle is situated close to its western edge, near the equator. The supercontinental arrangement results in extraordinary weather conditions and the Chinle is prone to 'mega-monsoons' that lead to particularly heavy rains and catastrophic flooding during the wet season. Humidity at this time is persistent and very high. This makes for very uncomfortable hunting conditions; without the proper clothing, immersion foot, crotch rot, bacterial and fungal infections and leeches can be a problem. Well-sealed waterproofs are considered vital.

Between the monsoons, the dry seasons can be harsh and incredibly hot, although many rivers and lakes remain well watered enough to run throughout the year.

GEOGRAPHY AND ENVIRONMENT

The high carbon dioxide, humidity and temperatures, as well as regular rainfall, mean that the Chinle is well vegetated; a floodplain fans out northwards from an cpciric body of watcr running north from the ocean. This floodplain forms a floodplain of numerous large rivers and lakes that fans out for thousands of square miles towards the Mogollon Highlands to the south and the Protorockies to the east.

The FOB is located in the well-forested southern foothills of the Mogollons while the reserve is away from the Chinle's interior heartlands and to the south of the range in rich coastal swamps and deltas. Like the interior, these deltas are well watered by numerous rivers, bayous and lakes. Gallery forests of large conifers, Araucarioxylons, overlook the rivers, braided streams, ponds and marshes; these trees can be massive, some measuring 200ft high. These thick forests of tightly packed, towering conifer trunks are dark and dank (especially in the wet season) and support few large animals.

The Araucarioxylons thin out away from the watercourses and are replaced by woodlands of smaller cycads and ginkgoes surrounded by beds of hardy ferns. During the wet season, larger herbivores will brave these fern prairies to feed on the new growth, followed, naturally, by their predators.

The rivers are lined with dense stands of huge horsetails that form the understoreys of the conifer forests. These horsetails can measure up to 100ft high and, in places, can be impenetrable. The ground covering is made up of various cycads, lycopods and club mosses, and ferns and mosses that can form coverings over the lower trunks of larger trees not unlike modern creepers and ivy.

The banks of the rivers can also be lined with thick mussel beds that can make the going underfoot difficult.

LICENSED TARGETS

You are licensed to hunt the following species in the Chinle:

POSTOSUCHUS

Length: 12–13ft
Weight: 500–600lbs
This heavily armoured carnivore is not a dinosaur, although it does have the appearance of how the likes of *T-rex* were envisaged in the early 20th century. *Postosuchus* belongs to a group of reptiles called Rauisuchidae, part of a group called

The Chinle's apex predator, Postosuchus.

the Pseudosuchia or 'false crocodiles' that does actually include modern crocodilians.

Undoubtedly the apex predator of the Chinle, its massive skull sports jaws are lined with long, serrated teeth adding to its dinosaurian appearance. The larger, less numerous teeth in the upper jaw are recurved to hook into prey. The lower jaw contains smaller but more numerous teeth, which act like the prongs of a fork, pinning the flesh of its prey while the large upper teeth slash and tear into it.

Postosuchus is equipped with large eyes and nostrils that provide excellent eyesight and sense of smell; it also has a

Jacobson's organ (more properly known as the vomeronasal organ or VNO); this allows the predator to 'taste' the air for particles of scent trapped in the humid air. In the dense forests and undergrowth of the Chinle, this gives the *Postosuchus* a great advantage while hunting.

Postosuchus is a facultative biped (like many herbivorous dinosaurs); it can move in both bipedal and quadrupedal gaits. The heavily built predator usually walks on all fours, although, with the forelimbs half the size of the hind ones, it is slow and cumbersome. However, when required to move somewhat faster, such as attacking prey, it often lifts itself on to its hind legs, using its considerable weight and mass to build up speed and inertia, the massive head counterbalanced by the long tail.

This is its primary form of attack. *Postosuchus* is an ambush predator. Its primary habitat is the thick gallery forests (where they are open enough to allow it to travel) and dense riverside understoreys. From concealed positions it will charge its prey, launching forward, propelled by its powerful hind legs to deliver a savage bite. As much of its prey is large, even larger than itself, this bite is not intended to kill. Blood loss and shock are often left to do that in smaller prey animals, but in larger ones *Postosuchus* uses microscopic allies to finish off the prey. It will trail its victim, sometimes for many days until infection takes its toll. It is the primary function of the VNO to track such infected prey; the VNO may also be used to sniff out the state of the infection.

Postosuchus' primary prey includes *Placerias* and Aetosaurs, even other, smaller Rauisuchids and Poposaurs; but in its role as apex predator, almost no animal is immune to attack except the larger Phytosaurs. *Postosuchus* is also a keen scavenger, stealing kills from any predator unable to withstand its bullying.

OPPOSITE: The huge phytosaur, *Redondasaurus*, ambushes the metopsaur amphibian, *Koskinonodon* — itself a pretty mean predator. All this action startles a freshwater xenacanthid shark.

Female individuals are generally larger than the males but the only real sign of dimorphism between the genders is the heavier armour of the males, probably as a result of sexual selection; the more numerous scutes and plates provide protection for males fighting for females and territory, while looking more impressive to prospective suitors.

Postosuchus is territorial. Male and female territories often overlap but the only time the animals socialize is during the mating season; otherwise, they are just as likely to fight with and scavenge from one another. Favoured territories include watercourses that remain wet throughout the year.

Breeding season for *Postosuchus* is at the start of the wet season, coinciding with the breeding season of many Chinle inhabitants; the start of the rains triggers mating. The pregnant females then begin fasting and make nests in deep forest. They stay with the eggs until they hatch, during which time they become particularly aggressive. A male *Postosuchus* will happily cannibalize eggs and young, and females will drive them out of their territory at any opportunity.

On hatching, the female continues to fast and protect the young long enough for them to disburse into the forest; from then on, her parental duties are over.

REDONDASAURUS

Length: 25ft
Weight: 2,200lbs

Without a doubt, the largest animal in the Chinle, *Redondasaurus* could easily be mistaken for a modern crocodile at a distance and in appearance, lifestyle and behaviour is not all that different to its modern counterpart. Its general body plan is very similar, even down to the same semi-sprawling gait; it is only in the head where significant changes make themselves apparent; the primary difference is that the nostrils are further back on the elongated jaws and set in a raised dome just ahead of the eyes (rather than in the tip of the snout as in crocodilians).

This feature is present in all members of the group that *Redondasaurus* belongs to: the Phytosaurs. This non-dinosaurian order forms the most common large family of vertebrates in the Chinle with numerous species adapted to several predatory ecological roles (ironically Phytosaurs were thought to be herbivorous when they were first discovered in the late 19th century and their name means 'plant lizard'). *Redondasaurus* is first and foremost a predator, as reflected in its teeth. Following a heterodont pattern that reflects, in evolutionary terms, its position as perhaps the most advanced member of the group, there is more than one tooth type; those at the tip of the long snout (which forms 80 per cent of the head length) are very long and interlock to form a perfect bear trap to capture prey. Behind the tip, the teeth are still long and conical-shaped; those at the rear half of the jaw are shorter but stouter, and better suited for crushing bone.

With a metabolism and body shape so like those of modern crocodiles and alligators, it is hardly surprising that the lifestyle and behaviour of *Redondasaurus* are very similar. It can regularly be seen basking beside Chinle watercourses, sunning itself or cooling off in the shallows, often with its jaws agape. It often gathers in larger numbers although these gatherings can be defined by age and sex, the largest conglomerations being those of young adults, again, like modern crocodilians. Such indolent behaviour and its apparently sluggish nature belie its abilities as an extremely effective ambush predator.

Its principal hunting strategy is to attack from the water; floating close to unsuspecting animals drinking or feeding by the water's edge, or charging from a well-chosen ambush site (always beware of deadfalls or dense riverside foliage). However, *Redondasaurus* adults can kill and eat just about anything living in the Chinle; from the largest *Placerias* and Aetosaurs to other predators, including smaller Phytosaurs. They hunt in the water, taking Metoposaurs, coelacanths, lungfish and freshwater sharks; but are not afraid to leave the water to scavenge or even attack slow or injured animals. Like modern crocodilians, they can put on a fair turn of speed with their semi-sprawling gait. However, unlike them, *Redondasaurus* does not leave its prey to decompose before eating; the heterodont tooth pattern enables it to break down carcasses quickly and efficiently.

The back and flanks of all Phytosaurs sport rows of armoured scutes and long dermal plates but this is especially true of *Redondasaurus*. However, with adults having no natural enemies to speak of, the armour is more for protection against the bites of its own kind. Many bear battle scars, usually as the result of squabbles over meals, as well as mating and territorial disputes. Some of these wounds can be very serious; the loss of a limb, broken jaws, blinded eyes.

COELOPHYSIS

Length: 10ft
Weight: 50lbs

The only truly iconic dinosaur of the Chinle, *Coelophysis* is a small opportunist predator with the basic body plan of most small dinosaur predators: the slim, athletic build with long tail, body and legs, relatively long neck and smaller forearms equipped with grasping hand. The hand actually dates *Coelophysis*; it still poses a rudimentary fourth finger, a primitive condition lost in most later Theropods who had three or even two fingers (Abelisaurs being the exception, as they too retained the fourth finger as a primitive feature).

The head of *Coelophysis* is slender, lightly built and narrow, the jaws carrying a large number of small teeth. It lacks a powerful bite, which narrows its choice of prey; it hunts mainly smaller animals such as insects, running Sphenosuchian crocodiles and the young and eggs of larger species. It will also fish for juvenile Phytosaurs and Metoposaurs, as well as fish and aquatic invertebrates, using its hands to pick over rocks and branches to scrabble for the likes of freshwater crayfish.

Sexually dimorphic, *Coelophysis* represents a body pattern that can be seen in many later Theropods. There are two forms; the female 'robust' and the male 'gracile', although the bland colouration of the females makes them quickly distinguishable from the more brightly coloured males, especially during the mating season. Both sexes have a covering of simple protofeathers not dissimilar to the down of a modern flightless bird. The down is constructed from the shaft that much later in Theropod evolution would support fully evolved feathers.

Generally, and especially during the dry season, *Coelophysis* is solitary and spends much of its time in deep forest close to water. However, the arrival of the wet season triggers the breeding season; pairs mate and nest in the gallery forests, both sexes feeding the precocial young who are soon ready to leave the nest. Once they are able to fend for themselves, the adults abandon them and the young scatter.

The breeding season also sees a more unusual behaviour pattern emerge in *Coelophysis*. The young adults that are too young to breed gather together in large flocks that are often joined by fully mature adults. This seems to relate to a

The little dinosaur, *Coelophysis*, hotly pursues breakfast — a Sphenosuchian crocodile — through a Chinle stream.

compulsion to migrate out of the more heavily forested areas and onto the fertile fern prairies. The newly watered fern prairie attracts a large number of animals including many young ones that provide a steady food source for non-breeding *Coelophysis*. The reason they form such flocks seems to relate to safety in numbers; so many smaller predators may deter or confuse larger ones as the dinosaurs travel out into open country. Once they have arrived on the prairies, the flocks quickly disband and the *Coelophysis* sweep the ferns for the rich plethora of prey before returning to the safety of the forest after a few days.

These flocks are vulnerable less to large predators than to natural disaster. Flash floods and forest fires have occasionally been known to wipe out hundreds of young *Coelophysis* in a single event.

The lightweight build of *Coelophysis* means that an elephant load will virtually obliterate your prey. We recommend a small, low-velocity round or flechette.

OTHER FAUNA

These sections are far from complete field guides; they are simply to give a broad outline of the kinds of animal you can expect to encounter in the various reserves.

PHYTOSAURS

As mentioned above, Phytosaurs are the most common vertebrates in the Chinle. They fall roughly into the three categories:

Fish-eaters: These species are similar to the modern gharial, with long, flattened, extended jaws containing many small cylindrical teeth ideal for a piscivore. The nostrils are well forward of the eyes, which are positioned to look upward so that the animal rests on the bottom and ambushes its prey from below. These species of Phytosaur, best represented by *Pseudopalatus*, have noticeable sexual dimorphism; the males have a raised nasal crest running from the eyes down the snout. These species are not considered particularly dangerous, unless provoked.

Generalists: These types, represented by *Smilosuchus*, have more robust snouts, with the nostrils in a raised crest (which also exhibits sexual dimorphism); the teeth are heterodont, including not just the cylindrical piscovorian type but also blade-like slicing teeth. They hunt a broader variety of prey, although this varies with age. The young are mainly fish-eaters but as they grow older their teeth adapt to hunting terrestrial prey and large aquatic types such as Metoposaurs. These types are considered dangerous and will attack without provocation.

Predatory: Represented by *Redondasaurus*. May be considered very dangerous.

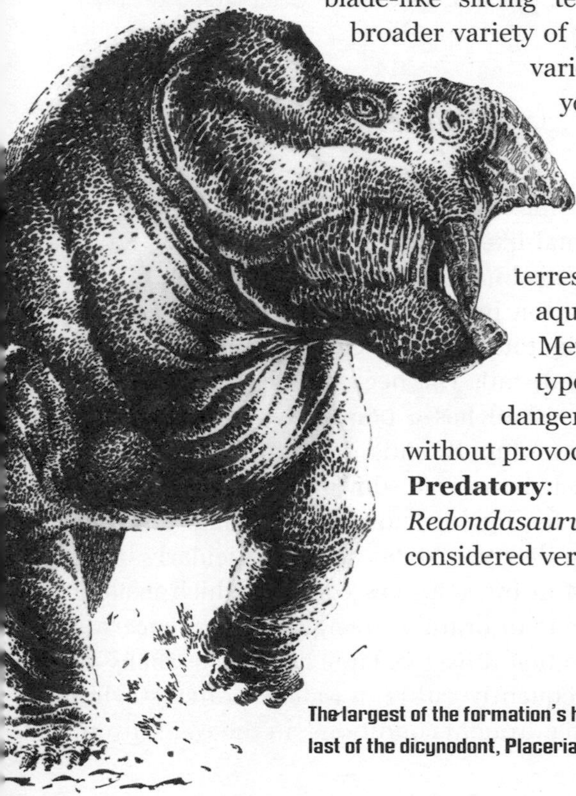

The largest of the formation's herbivores and one of the last of the dicynodont, Placerias.

CHINDESAURUS

Smaller (8ft long and 30lbs) but considered more dangerous than *Coelophysis*, *Chindesaurus* belongs to the Herrerasaurs, a group of dinosaurs better known from South America. This predator is lightly built but for its head, which is blunter and rather more solidly constructed than the slender, narrow skull of *Coelophysis*. Its teeth are long, serrated blades and adapted for delivering slashing wounds. Its hands retain the primitive four-fingered condition of *Coelophysis* (although the two are not closely related), but sport more robust claws, used to injure, handle and control prey. Not as nimble as *Coelophysis*, *Chindesaurus* is an ambush predator that can take larger prey than its counterpart.

PLACERIAS

The most common and the largest herbivore in the Chinle, *Placerias* is one of the last of the dicynodonts, a group of Therapsids (mammal-like reptiles) common in the Early and Mid-Triassic. This hippo-sized animal can be up to 12ft long and grow to a ton in weight. Its stout, barrel-shaped body is supported by four thickset legs and sports a stubby (and slightly comical) tail. The neck is thick and supports the large head; the skull has a bony crest running down between the eyes; the mouth ends in a powerful beak, on either side of which is a large, downward-pointing tusk. These are generally for digging and rooting through soil, but can also be used in defence. Males sport particularly large pairs that are used in intra-species combat, which usually involves little more than brutal shoving contests. *Placerias* is a social animal in that it lives in large herds of as many as a hundred. They frequently gather in wallows, often staying close to these during drought conditions; in the wet season, the herds nest colonially for mutual protection of the eggs and young. The young stay with the herd until they are big enough to form bachelor herds of juveniles. The adults migrate out of the more densely forested and wooded areas to feed on the new growth on the fern prairies; they return to the forests at the onset of the dry season.

AETOSAURS

The members of this strange order of quadrupedal, herbivorous Archosaurs are a relatively common sight in the Chinle. With their armadillo-like plated armour and pig-like snouts, they are forest foragers snuffling through the leaf litter for soft plant matter and even insects.

The largest and most heavily armoured of the Aetosaurs from this stage is *Desmatosuchus*. Large adults can be over 15ft long and 5ft tall at the hips. Unlike other contemporaneous Aetosaurs, they sport arrays of spikes culminating in a pair over the shoulder that can grow to 18in long. The spikes do prevent *Desmatosuchus* from foraging in thicker forest but the added protection means they can inhabit more open areas where large predators such as *Postosuchus* are more of a threat. They are generally solitary animals.

The broadest of the Chinle Aetosaurs is *Paratypothorax*. It lacks the bigger spines of *Desmatosuchus* but is easily identified by the line of short but hooked and flattened spines that edge its plated armour. *Paratypothorax* prefers swamps and marches, laying in mud or water, its broad back giving the appearance of a ridged stepping stone!

Stagonolepis grows to about 10ft in length and travels in small herds; it lacks the broad back armour of the two other types but this allows it to live in more thickly forested areas, where it travels in small herds of 5–20 animals. It also has better developed teeth than other Aetosaurs which, combined with the tough beak-like tip of its snout, allows it to crop tougher vegetation.

TRILOPHOSAURUS

These large iguana-like Diapsid lizards are a relatively common medium-sized herbivore that can reach a length of 7–8ft. The tip of their jaws ends in a tough, horn-covered beak while the back teeth are flattened and wide for crushing and grinding course plant matter.

There are other types of Diapsid lizards as yet unidentified but apparently closely related to *Trilophosaurus*. They differ primarily in that their diet is far broader and they will hunt and scavenge as well as browse on softer plants.

POPOSAURUS

Besides *Postosuchus*, a number of other predatory Rauisuchids inhabit the Chinle (although their exact relationship to one another remains unclear). These include *Poposaurus*: a large carnivore that can grow over 12ft and weigh up to 220lbs. It has small forelimbs and is an obligate biped, although, unlike dinosaurs, this has not helped with its speed. It is slow and ponderous, using a plantigrade posture (like a human's or bear, as opposed to the digitigrade structure of dinosaurs and birds). It is, in appearance, not that different to a bipedal Komodo dragon and just as carnivorous. It is an effective opportunist predator and scavenger; it will quite literally eat anything it can catch and consume any meat, no matter how decomposed. Avoid!

SPHENOSUCHID CROCODILES

These small, lightly armoured and nimble crocodilians are not much bigger than a house cat, averaging 2–3ft in length, much of which is tail. They are usually solitary and spend most of their time in the thick understoreys. Their erect posture makes them very fast in comparison to most Chinle Archosaurs, except *Coelophysis*, for whom these diminutive crocs are a regular meal. They forage for insects and small vertebrates; in the wet season they can be regularly found by waterways feeding on amphibian spawn and tadpoles.

METOPOSAURS AND OTHER AQUATIC HAZARDS

Metoposaurs are not, as their names might imply, reptiles; they are in fact very large and very common amphibians that can grow up to 10ft in length – imagine a more aggressive Japanese giant salamander. The most common forms are *Koskinonodon* and the smaller *Apachesaurus*. They are predatory by nature, having an alligator-like body plan, with broad, flattened heads, but with their eyes well forward on their heads. Their jaws are lined with a large number of small teeth, but much of their prey capture relies on suction, the jaws creating a surge of water into their mouths when they spring open that sucks small victims into the Metoposaur's gullet. These large amphibians are restricted to smaller prey, such as fish and crayfish, but will consume juvenile Phytosaurs and other small aquatic reptiles. They are generally solitary, spending most of their time on the bottom of ponds and streams, where their excellent camouflage, including an array of weed-like lobes lining the head, flanks and limbs, and a covering of detritus, makes them very hard to spot. They usually attack prey from below. They will bite unsuspecting hunters if stood on by accident so should you be required to wade rivers or ponds, beware.

In the wet season, large numbers of Metoposaurs gather in ponds and lakes to mate. These gatherings are noisy and the scene of much intra-species fighting between the males. The larger females lay hundreds of eggs in long strings of spawn, after which the gatherings disperse. The only other time Metoposaurs may be social is when they are compelled to be by circumstance: when the heat of the dry season withers away many of the watercourses they ply and they are forced together. Here, even the largest individual finds itself vulnerable to predators and scavengers.

Their aquatic habitat and large size tends to make Metoposaurs generally safe from predation but they are regularly prey for large Phytosaurs.

Other water hazards include Xenacanthid sharks; these strange, eel-like sharks only grow 2–4ft in length but have, on occasion, bitten an unwary hand. This is not a 'shark attack' as such, but most likely a case of mistaken identity in the murky waters of the Chinle.

CONCLUSION

The Chinle may be lacking in truly iconic trophies but there is no tougher, greater challenge for an experienced woodsperson. The dense cover and difficult terrain, the extremes of weather, from mega-monsoons to desiccating heat, and the harsh atmosphere all converge to make this an endurance trial for the hunter. Only the fittest, most dedicated team would choose this reserve but it is unlike any other environment on offer. It is the most alien and inhospitable, and if you really want to feel as if you truly are in another world, this is the one for you.

THE STORM

(Excerpt from Time to Die *by Jane Summers. Used with permission.)*

'Dust Off One Actual, Flamingo, Good morning. Comms check. How do you copy?'

'Flamingo, Dust Off One Actual, read you five by five. Over.'

The Dust Off crew would be in the alert five hangar, reading or gaming. Maybe cards, maybe some first-person shooter. The pilot could relax now. Settle in for a snooze.

'Red One Actual, Flamingo, Comms check. How do you copy?'

'Flamingo, Red One Actual, read you five by five. Over.'

The gunship crew would be equally indolent, enjoying the cool of the hangar, flight suits to the waist.

We, on the other hand, were exhausted. Two sweltering nights in and nothing to show but photos for our social media pages. We breakfasted on MREs and rehydrated with plenty of water. Whilst PJ cleaned and checked the weapons, I replaced the CO2 scrubbers on the rebreathers and topped off the air in the pony rig tanks with the compressor.

The shelter sweated even deep in the heart of the *Araucarioxylon* stand. It was cooler than being exposed to the Triassic sun, but the air was still and rich with the smell of resin. However, it had been too hot to sleep, despite the valiant efforts of the air con.

We didn't speak. Didn't need to. Went about our business through the medium of touch and instinct.

The final check was that our head cams were downloading to Mogollon FOB. They were, so we unzipped the shelter and stepped out into the morning.

Where light streamed through the trees at an acute angle, the air was yellow with a pollen storm. I blinked and tears welled. I pulled down my goggles. Haze swirled at the base of the giant conifers.

We still hadn't spoken beyond 'Good morning.'

I adjusted the rebreather mask. Sucked in clean, cool air. The clear plastic of the mask clouded when I breathed out. Sweat was already making my skin beneath the rubber seals damp. Beads of it ran from beneath the straps.

PJ hoisted his Benelli over his shoulder. Locked and loaded the shotgun. The cool of the ghillie suit contrasted with the air sticking to my forehead and cheeks.

The radio clicked.

'Flamingo, Flamingo, this is Mogollon. Weather update.'

PJ turned to me. Frowned.

'Mogollon, Flamingo, copy on weather update.'

'Yeah... the drone is showing a storm front coming in from the west.'

Boiling off the Protorockies and sweeping over the highlands.

'Copy, Mogollon.'

'Flamingo, we're issuing an advisory. How copy?'

'We copy loud and clear. Keep us appraised.'

'It's your dollar.'

'Copy. Out.'

We set off.

The shadows beneath the Araucarioxylons were dark and moist. The pollen clouds and dust added to the sensation that we were walking on the deepest of seabeds. Insects drifted slowly as the pollen, plankton in the air, through the shafts of deep yellow light.

The giant columnar trunks gave the forest the feel of a flooded temple, the roof a vault of deep green leaves overhead. We walked in a mosaic duff of dead needles. Dust hung like incense.

We weaved a trail between the conifers. A dark and brooding fairy-tale forest, the trees hemmed us in. There was a twinge of claustrophobia and the shadows threatened. But the very density of the forest precluded anything large enough to threaten us. Even so, my finger lingered on the trigger of my shotgun, its heft reassuring.

Finally, we could see sky. An iron white sky. The temperature rose. We made it to the deadfall, which had been predetermined as a navigational feature.

The thick covering of moss and curtains of tree ferns had browned away to desiccated dust in the drought but was still a blackish-green in the shadows. The dead Araucarioxylons had opened a hole in the canopy. Fighting for light, ginkgoes and cycads had grown up around the broken trunks and limbs of the giant conifers, felled by some ancient disaster. The western sky alluded to their fate. Billowing purple-grey thunderheads.

The field of ferns around the weathered trees were browned. Tinder dry. PJ rubbed leaves between his fingers. They crumbled to nothing.

'What do you think?' I asked. He looked west. Heat lighting flickered amongst the clouds.

'I don't know...' he drawled. 'I think we're far enough away from the watercourses to not have to worry about flash floods.'

'Wasn't thinking about floods... '

Lightning. Definitely, this time.

PJ hitched his rifle over his shoulder.

'Wanna head back?' I asked.

I didn't but the forest looked like it would burn faster than we could run or be rescued by the Pink Team.

I lifted the mask and sniffed. Just old wood and dry and earth. No smoke.

We pushed on.

Lycopods and club mosses give way to horsetails. We were close to the river. A hot breeze rattled the *Neocalamites*. They clacked together with a hollow wooden crack, like bamboo swords. They rose and thickened into an almost solid wall. The underbrush of ferns and club mosses was now a little greener, leaching the last of the moisture from the thick, muddy soil.

PJ stopped. Raised a fist.

We took a knee.

Again, the density of the horsetail thicket made a large predator unlikely but PJ brought the shotgun to his shoulder. Over the rustle of the harsh, hot breeze there came the click of the safety coming off.

I followed suit.

Something was coming. Needles crunched and wood crackled.

I drew a breath and waited.

The horsetails parted.

I let the breath out. It was an Aetosaur. *Calyptosuchus*. The armoured bear-pig armadillo-croc with a tiny head and broad porcine snout. Its back was raised into bands of flexible armour lined from neck to tail into ridges of bony scutes. It snuffled amongst the ground covering of ferns. Barged aside the smaller *Neocalamites*, rooting them out, upending them. Snorted up dust as it grubbed for roots. Would even take beetles or worms if need be. And right now, the need was great.

I lowered my weapon. PJ did the same. We smiled at each other as the delightful boar-sized armadillo-croc went about its business apparently untroubled by the presence of the two strange creatures regarding it. I snapped pictures.

But the *Calyptosuchus* had attendants. Following out of shadowy depths of the horsetails, elegant Silesaurs. Habitually four-legged but fast runners on two, they looked like pre-pubescent supermodel Sauropods, slim and rangy with long tail, legs and neck, and a little head. However, Silesaurs were not dinosaurs, just early experiments in the body plan. They trailed Aetosaurs to snap up whatever they stirred up or left behind, the scraps of plants they could never forage without the great digging claws of the armadillo-crocs getting at them first.

They waited patiently while the *Calyptosuchus* snuffled and I admired the prettiness of their gracile forms. I recorded footage for my Tumblr until finally the Aetosaur moved on. The Silesaurs darted to the bowl he had carved but there was nothing worth eating and they moved on with him.

We pushed on down to the trail. Found the tree we had marked the previous day and ducked under the deadfall slumped across an arroyo. Our footprints were still in the cracked rind of mud turned from terracotta to beige by the fall of pollen. My own face was filmed with it. The air was a deep, resplendent lemon and the light playing through the trees fell into beautiful gossamer curtains.

I sipped water from my camelBak as we plunged into the wall of horsetails. Dragonflies darted overhead, big and a glistening scarlet. *Neocalamites* and banks of *Equisetites* rose over us, swaying gently, the soft smack of wood on wood, and the rustle of ferns giving a soft, oriental ambience to the day. Something darted through the shadows ahead but was too fast for an ID.

Finally the giants gave way to more moderate-sized horsetails and wilting *Clathropteris* no thicker than a drumstick. The river was before us.

The pollen storm was thinning which meant we could see to the west. The storm there was building. It was a beautiful-ugly sky. Lightning slithered down and we counted to three before we heard distant thunder.

The radio clicked.

'Flamingo, Mogollon. Weather check.'

'Copy, Mogollon. Weather check.'

'Flamingo, that weather front is really starting to threaten. I'm putting the Pink Team on alert five. How copy?'

'Copy loud and clear. Any flooding?'

'We're not seeing anything from the drones. We've got them working the major watercourses and will keep you advised but if the weather deteriorates any further, we may lose coverage all together and be forced to ground the Pink Team, over.'

I glanced across to PJ. He just shrugged.

'Copy Mogollon.'

'Flamingo, we're also worried about fire at this point. Seeing a lot of lightning. We think fire would be the more likely threat right now. There are strong westerly gusts ahead of the front that could really drive it.'

We stood in silence. PJ toed the cracked earth.

'Flamingo? D'you copy?'

'We copy.'

'Flamingo, we're just warning you that the window to come and get you out is starting to close pretty fast.'

'How long do you think we have, Mogollon, over?'

A couple of heartbeats passed.

'I'd say you have maybe three hours. Max. How copy?'

'Copy, loud and clear.'

I looked at PJ. He pulled back his rebreather mask and rocked his head from side to side to loosen his stiff neck. Pushed a hand through his hair. Sweat made it greasy and black.

He snapped the mask back on. 'I reckon we can get to the wallow in an hour. The ground is open. They can pick us up from there.'

Made sense. I told Mogollon.

The guy at the other end didn't sound convinced but once more pointed out it was our dollar. I imagined the Mogollon crews shaking their heads in contempt at the *laissez-faire* attitude of the rich jerks who came back here to hunt and prove the manhoods they held so cheaply in the boardrooms and squash courts and wine bars they infested. As a woman, I wondered if they felt more or less contempt for me. Still, they were paid well to keep us alive and we were good tippers.

We hit the river and followed the right fork, the path less followed. The path not followed at all. Why, I don't know. Considering the time frame we were on, the left, the one we had followed yesterday and the day before, the one we knew better, would have taken us to the wallow faster, made more sense. It was broad and easily navigated.

But PJ, shotgun held forward more like a torch, led the way to the right and I unquestioningly followed.

The fork here was actually wetter. The waters were sluggish and little more than liquid mud, but it was standing, not just little more than wet riverbed flanked by dried out beds of crazy-paved earth, curled and peeling. But we soon found the going hard. The riverbed was beset by deadfalls. Conifers and ginkgoes eaten alive by fungus had collapsed. Tangles of dense brush had become snarled around them, and dammed the stream into ponds. Some pools were little more than chocolate-thick mud; some were fetid and stagnant, where every footfall released stinking clouds of marsh gas that I could smell even through the rebreather. Where the banks were dry, the ground was gravelly or beds of dead mussels that crunched beneath our boots.

And it wasn't just the water that was stagnant. The air was cloying and thick. The lifeless groves of horsetails and club mosses bent in and made the river a haunted tunnel.

Lightning flashed down amongst the deadfalls. Seconds passed before thunder rolled.

The bright light lit up the dead. A large coelacanth rotted in the mud, trapped in one of the vanishing pools. There were fish skeletons crawling with maggots and swarming with flies. That particular vista remained a feature of natural disasters no matter the epoch.

It was hard to keep alert while struggling through mud and tangled brush. I called a stop.

'I think we should turn back.'

PJ studied the thick roots and the creeping ferns and mosses covering them. It was dark. Something splashed.

He sighed. 'Let's just get through here and we'll see how it looks. If it's bad, we'll call it in and get a pick-up.'

Gripped by the politics of denial, I tried the mud around me. Only the cool air of the rebreather hid the stench of rot and kept the flies from crawling into my nostrils.

'Cover me,' he said and began hacking through the deadfall with his machete. I sited down the shotgun into the shadows but all PJ shook loose was a little Sphenodont that darted into the underbrush.

Finally, he made a hole and we struggled through.

We both took a drink and surveyed ahead. The river widened and the sun beat down through gaping holes in the canopy. The breeze drove pollen and dust into a yellow haze that spiralled up through the clacking horsetails.

The riverbed here was deep. Or had been. It was now little more than a shrinking pool of greyish-browny mud. Trapped in it was a multitude of huge Koskinonodons. The huge crocodilian amphibians were covered in glutinous mud to protect their rubbery hides. Some gapped their broad, flattened jaws. Their eyes were coal-black in the mud and when they blinked, a nictitating membrane swept across them as they sank into their sockets. They had fleshy little limbs and long, flat tails; some of the Metoposaurs struggled in death throes, their limbs scrabbling in the muck, tails lashing and kicking up fans of mud. Others looked too exhausted to struggle, their jaws agape, but if one of the more mobile amphibians came too close, the jaws would crack shut and the offended *Koskinonodon* would hiss like a snake, or gargle. However, many of the Metoposaurs were dead. Some of those at the edge of the pool were caked in dried clay, cooked and desiccated. Others merely mummified skeletons. A few, however, were freshly dead. The great predators were out of their element and easy pickings for scavengers. Large, iguana-like Diapsids tore at a fresh carcass. Their scaly heads were coated in blood and gore, and surrounded by a fog of flies. Darting about the lumbering saurians, nimble Sphenosuchians, dog-like and dog-sized, with long legs and slender tails. They snapped up scraps and irritated the huge Diapsids as they cantered about the charnel hole. Two squabbled over the remains of very large lungfish until they were driven off by the bigger scavengers.

We chose to go wide.

We were stopped in our tracks by the horsetails being forced apart by a nasty-looking customer. Both of us went for our shotguns.

It was a huge and very inappropriately named Poposaur.

Chest-high on us, it looked like how popular culture used to imagine a *T-rex*: ugly and bulky and plodding, with sad little arms and a massive, brawny head armed with giant jaws.

It announced its presence with a gurgling, wet roar and padded quickly – or as quickly as it could – at a Metoposaur. The amphibian, weak and exhausted, could do little but gape its jaws but it was a sad little deterrent and the Poposaur merely stepped around it as the *Koskinonodon* floundered.

The brutally ugly Rauisuchian tore a mouthful of mud and flesh, the Metoposaur hissing asthmatically.

The little Sphenosuchians came trotting over, hoping for odds and ends.

While the Poposaur ate the *Koskinonodon* alive, we stepped lively and went wide to avoid trouble. PJ stepped in the rotten carcass of something dead beneath the mud and had to drive off an intrigued Diapsid that came lurching towards him, its lashing tail kicking up clods of wet earth.

Further on, the stream narrowed and we once more faced another temporary dam of broken and twisted conifer branches and horsetail trunks. We struggled through and found a pond, shallow and stinking. Fish struggled at the surface, gasping for oxygen; coelacanths, little sharks, teleosts I didn't recognize.

A little gharial-like *Paleorhinus* lounged at the edge of the pool, dappled by a pink light coming in through the thick canopy that had closed around us overhead.

Lightning forked. Thunder rolled.

I checked the time and our position on the GPS. The hour's walk to the rendezvous was almost up and the wallow was still a klick away. Too late to make any planned pick-up. A jungle penetrator from the tilt-rotor could probably have pulled us out so my concerns were still only mild ones, but I checked in anyway.

'How's it looking?'

'Angry,' said the anxious voice from Mogollon. 'We're about to lose low drone coverage imminently. The Pink Team is prepped for dust-off but the window is closing pretty fast and I think you need to get ready for an evac. If the front passes, you can head back out tomorrow.'

'We'll push on to the wallow,' said PJ. 'They can pick us up from there.'

Lightning flashed.

The air was leaden and wet. I checked the rebreather scrubbers. Still 75 per cent efficient. And the tanks in the pony rigs were full.

The hot breeze became wind and I had to clear pollen and dust from my goggles. The high wall of *Neocalamites* around us shuddered and swayed. The stream *really* narrowed now and the shadows deepened. PJ kept stopping to survey the darkness, the hollows and dark dells where the horsetails were thickest.

We saw a long tail skitter away at one point but nothing else other than dead and dying fish trapped by the drying stream.

Then, up ahead, the banks once more widened and the colour in the air changed from a dingy dark green to a yellowy-pink, a haze swirling as the wind picked up again. The sky overhead was still a patchy blue, but the cloudy vanguard of the storm was streaming westward.

I checked the GPS again. We had made the wallow.

'Mogollon, Flamingo. We've made the wallow. How we doing?'

'Flamingo, Mogollon. We got a fire advisory. Looks like heat lightning has triggered forest fires to the east. It's forming a front with a speed right now of about four miles an hour. That gives you ... about five hours before it arrives. It may pick up speed but the storm might start laying down rain and blow it out. We'll check water levels, but so far, so good. Also registering a lot of lightning strikes.'

'Copy, Mogollon. So how long before the Pink Team might be grounded?'

'Wind's making it choppy already. If the fire takes a hold, smoke and vis will become the issues. Either way, I'd like you outta there within the hour.'

'What about our gear?'

'May have to leave it to fate, Flamingo.'

PJ shrugged. 'We got spares.'

'OK, Mogollon. We'll hole up at the wallow hide and wait for your pick-up. Keep us appraised.'

'Copy, Flamingo. We're launching the Pink Team and they'll set up an orbit west of you. Will keep you advised. Mogollon out.'

We edged cautiously to the wallow. Something was moving up ahead. In fact it was many somethings. A whole herd of them, each one weighting a ton or more, a dozen feet long. PJ looked back and smiled at me. We edged into the thickets of club mosses and tree ferns this side of the wallow's edge. There were deadfalls of horsetails steamrollered down, many hollowed out and moaning in the wind blowing through them. The hide was opposite, invisible, but PJ signalled we hole up and settle in.

We found a good spot. Plenty of cover. I took out my scope.

The *Placerias* herd was very impressive, even though many of its members looked thin and sickly. The size of hippos, their skin around their barrel-shaped bodies was leathery and folded, their limbs bandy, semi-sprawling. There was something pig-like about the heads, although the raised ridge on their skulls was more reminiscent of the sagittal crest on a gorilla's skull. They had beaks like a parrot or a turtle, and on either side was a downward-pointing tusk, scuffed and worn flat in the older animals. A few *Placerias* dug about with them, not to eat but to find water. One or two had been successful and they drank from the shallow wells, dribbling mud and sieving out what detritus they could. A squabble erupted as the biggest fought for possession of the waterholes. They cracked heads and wrestled with their beaks and tusks, shouldered and butted one another in tests of strength while the smaller and weaker animals stood at the edge of the wallow looking dead on their feet, ribs jutting, skin taut across their flanks. Several sat or lay on their sides. Probably close to death. They had already caught the attention of scavengers, Rauisuchians not unlike the Poposaur we had seen earlier but smaller and of an indeterminate genus. A pair, one much smaller than the other, picked over one of the inert, mud-caked *Placerias*, flicking a forked tongue over the dicynodont's rump. When it elicited no response, the larger Rauisuchian gave a tentative bite. That did trigger a response, the *Placerias* starting and snorting enough to send the Rauisuchians scurrying to a safe distance.

PJ had slipped his rifle from its case and set it up on the stout trunk of a fallen *Neocalamites*. Out of habit I checked wind speed and direction. Two knots. Westerly. But if he was taking a shot here, the breeze was not really going to have any impact at all.

I checked my watch. We had about 35 minutes. I was about to tell PJ when he said, simply, 'Look.'

There was a flash of lightning and only a brief interlude before thunder crashed. I followed his pointing finger.

My first dinosaur. A *Coelophysis* stalked out of the horsetails, sending a *Hesperosuchus* on its way, the little dog-croc trotting off to a safe distance.

I took photos. There was indeed an avian grace to the dinosaur, its head nodding, hips swaying as it followed in the wake of a *Placerias* pulling a deadfall apart with its tusks. The *Coelophysis* reached high to snap up a dragonfly. Crunched it down, insect wings and legs splayed out on either side of the dinosaur's head until it tilted its head back and chugged down the insect's long body. As the Placerias' shadow moved on, the colours on the Coelophysis' head glowed iridescent, ultraviolet, in the sunlight, making 'it' a 'he'. The rest of its slender body was coated in dust and when he scratched at his ribs, little puffs of dust blew off him.

Then, on his long scrawny legs, he trotted after the mammoth dicynodont, perhaps to catch whatever the giant stirred up or perhaps to enjoy the cool of the shadow it cast.

'What do you think?' PJ asked.

He tracked the dinosaur with the scope. It seemed unconcerned when forked lightning crackled down. Glanced up briefly when the following thunder rolled overhead. The sky was bruising to yellows and pinks and purples and greys.

It would have been a legal kill but the *Coelophysis* looked so small, so puny, compared to the giant dicynodonts, even to the Rauisuchians still making a nuisance of themselves, that it didn't feel so much like a kill as putting it out of its misery (even though it was by far the most lively of the animals at the wallow). It almost felt like a waste of ammo and I wondered if PJ was just getting impatient to bag something, anything, especially as this would have been our first of the Big Three. The irony of the name was not lost on me as I watched the smaller of the Rauisuchians chase off the little dinosaur. It could easily have killed the *Coelophysis*. And even if we did make the shot, the scavengers would be on it long before we could actually get anywhere near the carcass to take samples and measurements.

Still, it was a legitimate target, and it was what we came here for.

'Do it,' I said.

PJ chambered a round.

I watched through my scope. 'Go for the heart.'

The *Coelophysis* was scratching at something in the dried mud. He dug at it with his taloned hands. His irises were slits in the harsh sun, but the scales on his snout glistened. Flies clustered around his eyes and the nostrils at the tip of his long muzzle. His down looked well groomed if ragged and coated in pollen and grit.

Then suddenly he was gone. I looked up from my scope. He was just a tail disappearing into the horsetails.

And now there was commotion. The *Placerias* were lowing and braying. The more sickly were struggling to rise and the scavengers were parting for a *Postosuchus* that came swaggering into the wallow.

Now that was more like it.

It was easy to imagine why, on its discovery, *Postosuchus* was offered up as an ancestral Tyrannosaur. Although this theory was quickly discarded, right now it was easy to imagine where the assumption had come from. It was an impressive beast. It stalked forward, not on all fours but with its smaller forelimbs hung down loosely. It gave no indication it was about to attack, was hungry, thirsty, agitated or relaxed. It just strode towards the *Placerias*, its alligator back, covered in plates of armour and ridged with scutes, held straight; the huge Carnosaurian head was ugly, a brow of hornlets over each eye, lumps of horn running down its scarred and battered muzzle.

The creature's jaws were closed but when any of the *Placerias* turned to face the predator, they swung open and long blades glinted in the sun, and its long tail swung back and forth as it broke into a trot.

One of the *Placerias*, a smaller one, apparently sick or starved or both, was still laid out in the wallow, its hide a jigsaw of dried mud. Asleep or exhausted, it struggled to rise, mud flaking off in little bursts.

The *Postosuchus* sensed weakness. Charged.

The morning sun lanced through the thunderheads and struck the killer obliquely, casting long shadows.

Beside me came the crack of the rifle. It was a small sound compared to the roar of thunder coming in from the east but it was a clean shot.

The express load hit the *Postosuchus* in front of the eye. I saw the entry through my scope but the huge Rauisuchian kept charging. I heard PJ cycle the rifle.

But, then, the animal swerved and tottered before lurching into the ground in a fantail of dried mud and dust. It skidded to a halt at the feet of the small *Placerias* who could only look on stupefied before it turned and trotted off as fast as its bandy legs could carry it.

PJ stood and beamed at me through his mask. I remember his face very clearly. A yellowish tinge from the pollen. Reddish from the dust. He had his goggles on his forehead. The skin around his eyes was clean but ringed with dirt and sweat. His hair was tangled and greasy.

I keyed the mic.

'Mogollon, Flamingo. Splash one.'

The comms fritzed as lightning cut across the sky.

Somebody said something but the thunder was deafening.

'Mogollon, Flamingo, repeat, splash one.'

'Copy, Flamingo. Good show.'

PJ swung the rifle on his shoulder and swung astride the horsetail trunk.

'Flamingo, Mogollon, break, break, break. Flying conditions are becoming untenable. We need to dust you off in five. Pink Team is already inbound. How copy?'

Maybe enough time for a couple of photos. No time to do any science.

'Copy loud and clear.'

PJ swung off the log.

'Wait,' I called, unslinging my shotgun. Still a lot of very dangerous critters out there. A rubber bullet might not deter a full-grown *Placerias*.

PJ waited on a rise at the edge of the wallow. Could have been a log. Could have been a bank of mud-covered debris.

But it wasn't.

Something rose out of the ground. Dried mud burst upwards and something massive, not unlike a tree trunk, swung round then split apart. Jaws. They took PJ about the waist and he yelled my name.

Placerias wallows were usually sited in areas free from major aquatic predators. The *Redondasaurus* might have wandered here looking for water. It could have been there for days, weeks, seeing out the worst of the dry season cocooned in thick mud. It looked like riverbed, all ridges and lumps and bumps. Looked too big to be animal. More like a tree. It didn't need to eat. Just wait out the drought. Maybe the storm had aroused it. Maybe it smelt water or maybe the *Placerias* were old enough or young enough or ill enough to stir its appetite.

Didn't really matter.

All that mattered was the Phytosaur, then the biggest animal I'd ever seen, shook its head and its tail came thrashing out of the earth in an explosion of earth that covered me.

My shotgun was in my hand and I fired. It was a wild shot. No aiming. It was stupid. I could have hit PJ but at that point it wouldn't have mattered as he was screaming now and well on his way to being dead.

There was pandemonium in the wallow. The *Placerias* were clearing out as fast as they could. There was dust and pollen and mud flying and swirling and billowing, a fog of dirt that covered my goggles. I wiped them off but then had to blink grit away. My eyes were already teary. I blinked hard. The Redondasaur was so large it was hard to make out what I was seeing. Just trains of scaly skin streaming past and a crocodilian leg.

I struggled to fight my way out of the deadfall. Whipping branches caught the shotgun's strap, tangled around my arm. I fought free, trying to keep my head over PJ's screams and the yelling of the Pink Team crews in my earpiece.

All I wanted to do was get a clean shot.

I stumbled over club mosses. Tripped. Fell.

Got to my feet and drew the shotgun up to my shoulder.

The Phytosaur was padding its way down the streambed.

PJ had stopped screaming. I sighted through the shotgun's ghost ring. There was nothing but a vast swathe of armoured back. A river of scutes and plates and scales winding its way through mud and dead plant.

I don't remember too much after that.

I had liked PJ. But not enough to kill the *Redondasaurus* out of any sense of grief or rage. It was one of the calculated risks you took. Went with the territory, as one of the advisors had told us.

I stood for a while, I think, until I had to bend double and cover my face to hide from the downwash of the tilt-rotor. In shock, I was led to the aircraft and sat looking out at the beige, cracked mud of the wallow.

As we lifted off, the scavengers were already swarming in to enjoy a rare meal of *Postosuchus*.

Jane Summers is a model and CEO of her own fashion company. She is unique in having visited every time zone available to MHC®. PJ Griffin was listed as deceased; although the Pink Team gunship visually IDed the Redondasaurus that killed Griffin, the body was no longer visible and rules of engagement prevented them from firing on the Phytosaur. Griffin's body was never recovered.

THE MORRISON FORMATION

Period: Late Jurassic
Age: Tithonian stage (152–150 mya)
Present location: South- and Mid-West USA
Reserve size: approx 7,500 square miles (about the size of Kruger National Park, South Africa)

CONDITIONS

By the Late Jurassic, the supercontinent of Pangaea had split roughly in two along a north–south divide, into the supercontinents of Gondwana to the south and Laurasia to the north. The Morrison was situated to the extreme west of the northern landmass and was closer to the equator than the position of modern North America.

Atmospherically, 'greenhouse' conditions were still prevalent, with carbon dioxide levels still several times higher than in pre-industrial modern times. These raised levels of CO_2 allowed the gymnosperm plant groups (pines, conifers, ginkgoes etc.) to grow faster than they do in modern times, with forests continuing to flourish when water supplies allowed. This allowed the Morrison to support high numbers of large to gigantic herbivores and their predators in levels much higher than in similar present-day pre-industrial environments (estimates vary between 25 and 40 per cent higher, based on Africa's Amboseli National Park).

However, global temperatures remained high; the Morrison at this time experienced a short wet season with temperatures averaging 20°C (68°F) but during the prolonged dry season, temperatures were 40–45°C (104–113°F).

For these reasons, training regimes for the Morrison also involve low-oxygen acclimatization and the mandatory use of rebreathers, although the conditions tend to be far less humid than in Chinle.

GEOGRAPHY AND ENVIRONMENT

The Morrison Reserve is set beneath the foothills of the Front Range, a range of mountains that runs west then swings to the south-east. These mountains create rain-fed waterways, including a number of large rivers that run to the north-east. Some of these actually interconnect with waterways draining off the Sundance Sea, an inland or epeiric arm running down from the polar north from the global Tethys Ocean.

At the base of the Front Range foothills, where the Morrison FOB is based, the rivers, many of which run years long, create a lush floodplain. The rich soil of these deltas supports gallery forests of ginkgoes, podocarps and *Araucarians* (monkey puzzle trees), which keep their leaves all year round, and conifers not dissimilar to modern redwoods, which drop their needles at the start of the dry season. The forest understoreys are formed by tree ferns and cycads and their close relations;

these are divided into slim, long-trunked types such as *Williamsonia*, that can grow to as high as 6–7ft; and the barrel-trunked types that look ostensibly like giant pineapples. The males of these types produce flower-like cones in the wet season. The ground covering is formed of varieties of fern and ground pine, while horsetails and scouring rushes grow densely along the edges of rivers and ponds.

These forests support populations of mid- and high-browsing Sauropods, the most common of which is *Camarasaurus*; they also include the uncommon and truly giant *Brachiosaurus*. These are largely non-migratory, although Camarasaurs do follow the rains north-east into more open habitats.

These well-watered floodplains give way to the Morrison Foredeep, the vast interior of the continent that is close to sea level and as such is poorly drained. The Foredeep is peppered with depressions created when the Earth's crust warped and folded millions of years before. These depressions create large lakes and saltpans. In the wet season, many of these lakes and salt flats fill up, often preceded by violent flash flooding.

The gallery forests of the floodplains give way to more open woodland the further you travel in to the Foredeep, much of which is covered by fern prairie, with the occasional hardy *Araucarian* and conifer to provide the only shade.

During the wet season, the reddish soil turns green with thick coverings of ferns; this triggers a massive migration of herbivorous dinosaurs, including large herds of low-browsing Sauropods.

However, the dry season leaves many watercourses parched, but some bayous and billabongs do remain watered through the year, and support local populations of hardier types, including *Camptosaurus* and *Stegosaurus*, and many smaller opportunist omnivores and herbivores such as the burrowing

Drinker and *Othnielia*; the burrows of the latter two can be a real menace and have accounted for many a broken ankle. These herbivores survive by browsing on the few plants capable of toughing out the dry season, or by digging for the seeds and tubers left dormant in the soil.

The big herds churn up the prairie so that once the dry season arrives, there is little left but a dust bowl; however, the herds do leave behind a rich compost of dung that provides fertilizer for the next generation of plants. By then, the herds will have dispersed and returned to the shade and cooler climes of the floodplain forests. Many species see out the dry season here, awaiting the rains that then trigger the rush to breed and fill the forests with hatchlings of many kinds and the fern prairies with crèches of young.

LICENSED TARGETS

You are licensed to hunt the following species in the Morrison:

ALLOSAURUS

Length: 30ft
Weight: 1,500–2,000lbs
Allosaurus is the most common of the Morrison predators. This species is often ascribed to *A. atrox*, but confusion amongst the *Allosaurus* classification means that this is by no means definitive.

By and large solitary, its body form is typical of most Carnosaurs; long tailed, shortish trunk and long, well-muscled neck. The skull is modest in length and while not as strongly constructed as in, for example, the Tyrannosaurs, the various bones of the skull are built to flex and bow, increasing the gape of the jaws (see below), and to withstand stresses imposed by struggling prey by flexing with forces exerted on it. The roof of the skull is thin (although *Allosaurus* generally holds its head horizontally, making a shot here problematic).

Allosaurus is easily recognized by the lacrimal horns over the eyes; these are more pronounced in males where they function as sexual displays as well as shading the eyes, a useful function in its favoured habit – the open fern prairies and woodlands of the Foredeep. There is also a pair of raised ridges running from the tip of the snout to the lacrimal horns. These and the head in general have striking black, white and red markings in male Allosaurs; females also sport markings around the eyes and on the upper jaw, but they are not as pronounced.

Allosaurus has large nostrils and sinuses incorporating Jacobson's organs (vomeronasal organ or VNO); this gives the animal an excellent sense of smell. They do, however, lack the binocular vision of later Theropods, stereoscopic vision being limited to no better than that of a modern crocodile; however, this is perfectly adequate for gauging the range of prey and timing its attacks. It's also possible that the more lateral placement of the eyes improves prey detection in the wide-open plains (a feature usually employed by herbivores to *avoid* predators!)

Allosaurus' hearing is focused on low-frequency sounds; this may help it detect the infra-sound created by Sauropods' digestion and communication, or their heavy footfalls (Ornithopods produce similar if less pronounced noises).

Allosaur teeth are classically modelled; large upper teeth and smaller lower ones. They are all serrated and have a blade-like construction. The jaws lack a strong bite force (less than a modern alligator) but can withstand powerful vertical forces and gape extremely widely. Although jaw muscles are generally reduced, the neck muscles are very powerfully developed. As such, while incapable of crushing bone, the jaws of *Allosaurus* operate very effectively as the serrated edge of a saw, cutting deep slashing wounds into prey when they are drawn violently back. Such wounds are generally not meant to kill but leave wounds that slow and disable larger prey.

The long legs (in Carnosaur terms) make *Allosaurus* relatively fast – certainly faster than most of its prey items – with an average speed of around 20mph although it can perform quicker bursts of speed. The forearms are short but very well muscled and equipped with three fingers, each sporting a large, curved claw.

All these features – the short serrated teeth, the flexing skull capable of withstanding trauma across the vertical axis, the wide gape, turn of speed, powerful forearms – make *Allosaurus* a very effective and active predator. Not an ambush predator as such, it stalks and chases prey, charging in and delivering slashing bites and wearing its victim down through shock and blood loss. Smaller prey such as Dryosaurs and Camptosaurs (its favoured food items) are sometimes dispatched in a single attack, the Allosaur using its superior weight and momentum to charge the prey down, then pinning it with powerful forefeet and arms. The victim is then dismantled across a vertical axis (like modern birds of prey), the head jerking upwards to pull the prey apart. The wide gape can remove huge chunks of flesh in one bite and Allosaurs consume large amounts of flesh in one sitting.

Favouring the open fern prairies, Allosaurs are opportunist daylight hunters of smaller animals. Prey is less abundant than in the southern woodlands and gallery forests; this is especially true in the dry season when it will sometimes take on larger animals including Sauropods. Generally it favours

THE MORRISON FORMATION

A blood-soaked, fly covered *Allosaurus* stand ankle deep in sauropod guts.

juveniles and sub-adults but it has been known to attack full-grown adults where it favours the smaller or lighter species such as *Barosaurus*, *Diplodocus* or *Haplocanthosaurus*. Such attacks are usually very long and agonizing affairs, with the Allosaur conducting a number of attacks over a period of days in the hope of eventually exhausting the Sauropod into fatal submission. Many Sauropods carry the scars of failed attempts.

Allosaurus is also quite capable of taking on armoured dinosaurs. As it shares its habitat with *Stegosaurus*, this iconic dinosaur is regular prey for Allosaurs. However the Stegosaur's famous 'thagomizer' makes it very dangerous prey and, as with larger Sauropods, attacks can be protracted and exhausting for both combatants; so adult Stegosaurs are taken only if the Allosaur is very hungry.

Smaller Ankylosaurs such as *Mymoorapelta* are rare prey, living mostly in gallery forests as they do. However, some hardier species scratch out a living in the billabongs of the Foredeep. These tough little types are pugnacious and well armoured, and an Allosaur's only hope of killing one is to flip it on its back – never an easy task at the best of times.

Allosaurus is very territorial, with home ranges extending hundreds of square miles and usually centred on a permanent water source. Favoured territories are those that include migration routes for herds moving out into the Foredeep during the wet season. Male and female territories do overlap but they remain aggressive to one another outside of the breeding season. Intra-species battles are frequent occurrences, most often triggered by territorial intrusions but also by the contesting of kills, especially during the dry season when hungry adults are drawn to the circling pterosaurs that tend to gather over a kill. This is also the time when many juveniles and sub-adults may find themselves cannibalized by adults.

The mating season is triggered by the arrival of the rains.

Colours brighten at the season's start in a male of breeding age; he will mate with all females who enter his range. Males roaring to attract a mate herald the start of the mating season.

Pregnant females, especially those with overlapping territories, will gather into packs. They hunt together in a rare display of social behaviour which allows them to fatten up quickly before they dig out their nests together. Such colonial nesting allows for mutual protection from predators (including male Allosaurs). They can contain two to five females; this allows one or two to remain on guard duty while the others hunt. The eggs hatch very closely together. The chicks are precocial and leave the nest soon after hatching, the clutches forming a single crèche protected by the mothers. They stay together until the young fledge. The independent juveniles are long-legged; they are far faster than the adults and prey primarily on small, fast Ornithopods.

While *A. atrox* is the one recognized species of the genus *Allosaurus* at this time in the Morrison, it is possible that a giant species is present, although this has yet to be verified. There have been scattered reports of huge Allosaurs in the foothill forests of the Front Range; these may be specialist giant Sauropod hunters previously described as *Epanterias* or *Saurophaganax*. However, they could be just very large specimens of *A. atrox* whose size has resulted in a behavioural change, allowing them to prey on the largest Sauropods that are restricted to the thick southern forests.

TORVOSAURUS

Length: 30–35ft

Weight: 2 tons

The largest of the Morrison Theropods, *Torvosaurus* is also far less common than *Allosaurus*, being largely restricted to the deeper woodlands, gallery forests and foothills of the

Front Range, although sub-adults have been seen far out in the Foredeep.

While only slightly longer than *Allosaurus*, *Torvosaurus* is far more robust and rugged. Its head is long and narrow, with a slight kink above the nostrils. The teeth are blade-like, those in the premaxilla protruding slightly. There is a lacrimal horn but it is far less pronounced than in *Allosaurus* and *Ceratosaurus*, but does flair to horizontal, where it functions as an effective sun shade. The rest of the body is by and large typically 'Theropod' although the body is narrow (a feature that may help it navigate thick forest with greater ease) and the long tail is held stiff and high, acting as a counterweight to the large head. One distinctive feature of *Torvosaurus* is the large thumb claw carried on its short but robust forelimbs; this is not unlike the dewclaw in big cats and is used like a crampon to hook into prey or, in the case of males, to secure a hold on the female during mating. With this in mind, females also have thicker skin around their shoulders and the base of the neck. The dewclaw often leaves scars on the female *Torvosaurus*.

Females are larger and more robust than the males. Both have markings across their bodies patterned in an 'aeluroid' style, with spots and speckles set in broad 'clouds' of colour to break up the animal's silhouette when moving through the sun-dappled interior of woods and forests. The males, however have very pronounced 'go faster' flame-coloured markings on their heads, making them very recognizable.

Torvosaurus is solitary except during the mating season. Its forest and woodland habitats have high prey densities year round: in the wet season, *Camarasaurus* and *Brachiosaurus*, and their young, and larger *Camptosaurus* species; in the dry season migratory Sauropods such as *Apatosaurus* and *Haplocanthosaurus*, the occasional *Stegosaurus longispinus*

Portrait of a battle-scared *Torvosaurus*.

and even Ankylosaurs. This means that individual Torvosaur ranges aren't as big as those of an *Allosaurus* out on the less prey-rich fern prairies.

Primary prey for *Torvosaurus* is mid- to large-sized Sauropods, the most regularly taken being *Camarasaurus*, certainly the most common of the Morrison's Sauropods. Typically an ambush predator, a Torvosaur's primary strategy is 'long-term pursuit and harassment'. It is mainly a daylight hunter but will use the fading light of dawn or dusk to cover attacks. Charging from cover, it will inflict long, deep wounds on its victim with its jaws and dewclaws, especially on the hind limbs, forcing the Sauropod to move more slowly and fall behind the relative safety of the herd. The Torvosaur stays close and over a period of days inflicts more and more bites, steadily weakening the prey until it is able to start feeding, usually while the shocked prey is still alive. (This is usually the best tracking strategy in finding a *Torvosaurus*: follow the blood trails and where possible, find the injured prey and stay with it until the Torvosaur makes another attack.)

Torvosaurs breed in pairs that could be life-long matings although this needs further study. The female seems to live in the same broad territory that overlaps with several males; the one she chooses to breed with stays with her to raise the brood of chicks, both sharing nesting and hunting duties. The chicks are less precocial than in *Allosaurus* and *Ceratosaurus*, staying in the nest where bigger chicks will kill and cannibalize the smaller ones.

Raising chicks sees adults broaden their menu to incorporate anything they can catch and kill; hatching is usually timed to the mass Sauropod hatchings, when small prey is abundant. Torvosaurs are opportunist scavengers, driving other predators from their kills as frequently as possible, but during the breeding season they make much greater use of their more muscular frames and aggressive temperaments.

On leaving the nest, the chicks are attended by both parents until they fledge, at which point the adults abandon them and return to a solitary existence through the long dry season. The fledgling Torvosaurs follow the young Sauropods into the deeper forest, although they are as likely to fall prey to small Carnosaurs and to Coelurosaurs such as *Ornitholestes*.

CERATOSAURUS

Length: 20ft
Weight: 1,300lbs
The third in the triumvirate of great Morrison predators is also perhaps the most enigmatic; it is certainly the rarest and, with its impressive head ornamentation, the most sought after.

Generally restricted to deep forest and open woodland,

Ceratosaurus could also be termed semi-aquatic, spending far more time in water than any other non-crocodilian predator, and including in its menu large fish (especially giant lungfish) and crocodylomorphs of many kinds, both terrestrial and semi-aquatic types. It will also take large prey, such as small Sauropods, Camptosaurs and Stegosaurs.

Ceratosaurus is easily recognizable by its distinctive flattened nose horn at the end of its snout. There is also a pair of hornlets over the eyes not unlike those in *Allosaurus*. These horns are not just for show and for shading the eyes. In *Ceratosaurus*, the horn is used in intra-species battles, mainly between the males during the breeding season, following highly stylized and noisy threat displays.

Ceratosaurus, the rarest and most enigmatic of the Morrison's Big Three.

The roughly rectangular head is armed with rows of very large teeth; these can not only inflict ghastly slashing wounds in large prey but are also useful in snaring more slippery aquatic prey as well as puncturing the armoured scales of the biggest lungfish.

Ceratosaurus is unique amongst the large predators in that it will hunt by night; as such its vision and sense of smell are acute. Its long body and longer, deep and flexible tail are ideal for weaving through thick forest but also make *Ceratosaurus* an excellent swimmer. The spine is marked with a line of oestoderms – raised scales that run the entire length of its body, from the base of the skull to the tip of the tail. The legs aren't particularly long and it is not built for speed; the arms are very small and carry a reduced fourth finger.

Sexual dimorphism in size and build is generally less exaggerated than other Theropods, but the male is strongly marked, the body a blue-black with white stripes, and white socks on the lower legs and the head. The female is a rich brown or tan and has fewer stripes.

Mating season for *Ceratosaurus* takes place at the end of the dry season. The male's sperm is retained in the female's cloaca until the rains arrive, when the eggs are fertilized. She then builds a large nest mound, usually close to water, into which she lays the eggs then guards them until they hatch. Ceratosaur eggs gestate longer than other Theropods and the young are born precocial. They are abandoned very quickly by the female but the young can swim from an early age and will eat anything they can catch, from insects to small fish, frogs and salamanders and even other baby dinosaurs. They therefore have very large and effective teeth from a very young age.

OTHER FAUNA

PREDATORS

Ceratosaurus is rare but there are two other Theropods even rarer. *Stokesosaurus* and *Marshosaurus* are two predators of indeterminate classification. Little is known of them and sightings of them are scant. Both are small but definitely not Coelurosaur-like; one seems to live in the thick gallery forests of the Front Range while the other has been seen twice out in the far ranges of the Foredeep. It is not even certain which species is which but the forest type is definitely feathered.

More common are the Coelurosaurs, particularly *Coelurus*, *Ornitholestes*, and *Tanycolagreus*. These swift predators generally hunt small, fast prey as large as *Dryosaurus* but also running crocs, Nanosaurs, mammals and the young of other, larger dinosaurs. The smaller types, *Coelurus* and *Ornitholestes* are lightly built and represent little threat to hunting teams, both growing no more than 8ft and 40lbs. However, *Tanycolagreus* is a larger animal, over 12ft long; it preys principally on small to medium-sized Ornithopods, but is a major threat to hunters on foot in open woodland and the interior of the Foredeep.

SAUROPODS

The most important members of the Morrison fauna are the Sauropods. Massively impressive to look at, they also have a profound impact on the landscape. With as many as half a dozen species of these thunder lizards, some travelling in large herds at certain times of year, they can cause catastrophic damage to woods and forests. The biggest can bulldoze great trails through the thickest forest, forcing down old growth conifers. However, in doing so, they open up understorey species to the sun and allow dormant seeds to germinate and replace the fallen gallery forest giants; this also forms new habitats for smaller Sauropods and Ornithopods. These giant herbivores also leave huge amounts of dung to act as compost and fertilizer for the new growth.

All the Sauropods breed more or less together. Males of all species have long dewclaws and like Theropods use them to stabilize themselves during mating; accordingly, females also have thick skin and in some cases armour over their shoulders to protect themselves, although many carry mating scars.

After mating, pregnant females move into the forested foothills and gallery forests to make simple nests, which vary from species to species, ranging from simple hollows with the eggs laid in a spiral, to more sophisticated mounds of vegetation. Some smaller species such as *Camarasaurus* and *Diplodocus* nest in rough colonies in more open woodland, but usually close to denser forest and permanent watercourses.

However, no matter the laying strategy, no matter the species, the eggs are all timed to hatch at night. This mass hatching means no one species is singled out for attention by predators.

Known species include:

Apatosaurus: Grows to about 70ft long and weighs to 30 tons (although larger individuals may be present). *Apatosaurus* is an opportunist feeder, browsing both horizontally at low level and in the vertical axis by adapting a tripodal posture, using its tail as a crutch to allow it to reach high into the tree canopies. It is, by and large, solitary in all stages of growth, but also very widespread, being tough enough to withstand the extremes of the fern prairie but robust enough to shoulder its way into deeper forest. Males fight in the tripodal stance, using their very large dewclaws as weapons in territorial and breeding disputes; this posture, together with the large dewclaws, also makes for an effective deterrent against predators. Breeding-age adults gather at the edges of the Foredeep for courtship and mating at the end of the dry season; pregnant females migrate into the woods and forests to lay their eggs in simple trench-like nests amongst dense understoreys; these are abandoned on laying. The males often stay out on the Foredeep, foraging on the wet season's new growth of ferns; many head into the woods and forests for the dry season.

Diplodocus: Grows up to 90ft and weighs 10–15 tons; however there are a number of very large individuals (usually males) over 110ft that have been sighted; these 'supersaurs' are not a separate species but just very large and very old individuals.

The most common Sauropod of the Foredeep fern prairies and more open woodlands, with its long, almost-horizontal neck and its narrow head and peg-like nipping front teeth, *Diplodocus* crops and strips off low vegetation, although it can adopt a similar tripodal stance to *Apatosaurus* if hungry enough (as with the latter, this stance is used in intra-species combat and to deter predators).

Mating and breeding follow the pattern of most of the Sauropods, although *Diplodocus* females migrate into the Front Range highlands and gather in loosely associated colonies to nest in open woodland. These colonies are often close to denser brush and forests, which provide the young with a chance to make cover when they hatch. Unlike forest-nesting species, *Diplodocus* eggs hatch at dawn so that the big-eyed young have a chance of seeing and smelling the forests nearby.

The teeth arrangement of the young is very different to the adults, allowing them to feed on a broader menu of plant types, thereby fuelling their rapid growth rates. The juveniles usually stay in cover for a number of years until they are large enough to form into age-specific unstructured herds of juveniles and risk more open ground. These herds tend to travel out into the Foredeep where the young graze on the fern prairies in the wet season and move back into the woods and forests in the dry season. These juvenile herds are a common sight in the Morrison. The young are also quite aggressive to predators, rearing up or using the legendary 'whiplash' tail of the Diplodocids (to which *Apatosaurus* and *Barosaurus* belong) that, as the name implies, is used to lash out at predators as a deterrent.

Barosaurus: Grows up to 85ft and weighs about 22 tons. *Barosaurus* is instantly recognizable by its extraordinarily long neck but has a more slender build than *Diplodocus* and tan and beige markings. The long neck has broad lateral but little vertical movement; it is most definitely a low-grazer and spends most of its time in open woodland or the interior of the Foredeep especially during the wet season, where it generally feeds on ferns and cycad and tree fern crowns. It is far less common than its Diplodocid relatives and travels in small herds or alone.

Nesting usually takes place by permanent watercourses lined with riverine forests that provide cover for the newly hatched young. Hatchlings are born with much shorter necks and are similar to *Diplodocus* young in diet.

Like other Diplodocids, *Barosaurus* has a whiplash tail to deter predators.

Haplocanthosaurus: Grows up to 50ft and weighs about 12 tons. This is one of the smaller and the rarest of the Morrison Sauropods. It is also the most generalized and inhabits the

broadest range. Little is known of its habits and reproduction.
Camarasaurus: Grows up to 50ft and weighs about 20 tons. Herds of this Sauropod are a common sight in the forests and woodlands of the Morrison throughout the year, and at the edge of the Foredeep during the wet season. Although roughly the same size as *Haplocanthosaurus*, it has a far more robust build and more unusual body plan. While most other Sauropods have four equally sized limbs or slightly smaller forelimbs, *Camarasaurus* is raised at the withers, naturally deflecting the neck upwards. The head is also boxy and blunt-snouted, and the teeth are chisel-topped and spatulate-shaped – very unlike the narrow, refined heads of Diplodocids. These differences allow a separation in the ecology of these Sauropod types. *Camarasaurus* is a true browser, feeding principally in the vertical, high-browsing tree canopies as far as it can reach, its stout teeth breaking up twigs, bark and cones as well as leaves. Physiologically it finds it difficult to browse low or graze like the boom-necked Diplodocids, which restricts its range to woods and forests. *Camarasaurus* herds will enter the Foredeep but stay close to riverine forests or open woodland.

This species is also most responsible for the damage done to the forests and woods of the Morrison (along with, perhaps, *Apatosaurus*); herds will shoulder down smaller trees and strip the lower branches but this is vital in maintaining the health of the Morrison ecosystem.
Camarasaurus is a particularly aggressive Sauropod (be warned!); lacking a whiplash tail and limited in its ability to rear like Diplodocids, it will use its strong jaws and teeth to inflict a nasty bite.

Camarasaurs nest colonially in the highlands of the Front Range, often close to *Diplodocus* colonies, where the two species presumably offer mutual protection against predators.

Several Morrison inhabitants, including a Nanosaurus (in its burrow), a Dryosaurus (left), a pair of Camptosaurs and Camarasaurs. Meanwhile, a small terrestrial croc makes a dash for cover in the foreground.

The young spend their early years in deeper forest and wooded areas, swamps and marshes, growing fast but not reaching sexual maturity until at least two decades old. During this period, pre-breeding-age individuals form herds of similarly aged animals. *Brachiosaurus*: The likelihood of seeing one of these truly giant Sauropods – the biggest in the Morrison and one of the biggest ever – is remote as they live in deep conifer forests where they browse the very tallest of trees. These forests are largely outside the range of the hunting reserve, but special trips can be arranged to try to see one of these behemoths.

Killing any Sauropod is strictly forbidden unless deemed in self-defence. This may seem like stating the obvious but the sheer immensity and majesty of Sauropods make them tempting targets.

ORNITHOPODS

Stegosaurus grows to about 30ft in length and weighs about 5 tons. This iconic dinosaur is instantly recognizable and fortunately quite common in the Morrison. It's also the formation's largest non-Sauropod herbivore.

Stegosaurus is easily identifiable by the alternating row of plates that run across its back and down its tail. These are sexually dimorphic. The female plates tend to be smaller and more leaf-shaped, coming to a point on top; the male's are much larger especially over the hips, and more diamond-shaped. The latter's are also far more colourful and used in sexual display and threats. The female's plates represent a more defensive shape; they are boldly marked but more as a deterrent to predators.

Female Stegosaurs also tend to be smaller than the males but both sexes are equipped with thagomizers, the array of four tail spikes named after a famous Gary Larson *Far Side* cartoon. These spikes can measure as long as 3ft. The tail itself is structurally quite ridged but flexible at the base so that it can be swung horizontally with a flick of the hips, propelled by the animal's powerful back legs with their massive thigh muscles. Tactically, however, it's the forelimbs that do the work, pushing off and pivoting *Stegosaurus* around its hip-based centre of gravity, and keeping the thagomizer towards its attacker.

Generally a quadruped, it is also quite a capable biped. It will rise up on its hind legs as part of a threat display to predators (and, in the case of males, to rivals), and to browse the crowns of cycads and tree ferns. It is, however, primarily a low-browser/grazer, feeding on ferns, horsetails and ground pines. For this it uses its tough keratin beak to pluck off plant matter; the teeth are relatively simple and used solely to cut up leaves before they are swallowed into its fermentation vat gut.

Stegosaurus mating is a gentle, careful business, the plates a definite nuisance during sex. If you're visiting at the start of the wet season, it's worth trying to find a pair mid-coupling to watch this balletic display.

The female nests in deep shrub or forest, laying her eggs in a mound of vegetation; she stays with the eggs until they hatch then abandons the young. The hatchlings stay deep in riverine forests and dense understoreys; they also spend a lot of time in marshes and swamps, which provide a degree of safety from large Theropods and Coelurosaurs, but makes them vulnerable to crocodilians.

There is a possible second species of *Stegosaurus* very similar to the African Stegosaur *Kentrosaurus* (it may actually be a species of the latter). This smaller species is restricted to the deep forests of the Front Range highlands and is recognizable by its smaller plates, more numerous tail spines and a long spike over each shoulder.

ANKYLOSAURS

This family of armoured dinosaurs evolved in the Late Jurassic (although they are ironically named after one of its last members, *Anklyosaurus* – see below) and there may be two species in the Morrison but possibly more. The two known for certain, *Mymoorapelta* and *Gargoyleosaurus*, are roughly similar in size, growing to about 10–15ft in length and weighing about a ton. They differ in the type of armour although both have a paving of armoured scutes on their backs and flattened spikes running down their flanks. They also have armoured heads with small spikes extending from their cheeks and the back of their skulls.

These are hardy animals that will eat any kind of plant matter and even scavenge, should the opportunity present itself; they can also live for extended periods without water. As such, one species seems to live out in the Foredeep, eking out an existence around billabongs and waterholes on the interior during the long Morrison dry season. The other species lives in the thick gallery forests and swamps, living an almost semi-aquatic existence akin to the likes of a forest hog or pygmy hippo.

Rarely seen, little else is known about these dinosaurs.

CAMPTOSAURUS

The most common herbivore of the Morrison, the more widespread and smaller species grows to about 15ft in length and weighs about half a ton. The rarer giant species can measure 25ft and weigh over a ton. Both the lesser and the giant species move in herds; in the case of the former, these can be very large, more than 100 individuals. The giant type travels in smaller groups of five to ten animals. Young often travel with the adults for protection.

Both types have a typical Ornithopod-like build, with a small, beak-tipped head, barrel-shaped body and long neck and tail; they are habitual quadrupeds but semi-bipedal. This enables them to feed along a broader vertical axis. Generally a low-browser and grazer, they can stand to feed higher up if needed; this enables them to expand their diet during the worst of the dry season. The giant *Camptosaurus* has much longer, more heavily built arms and a thumb spike akin to later Iguanodonts. It will use its greater size and powerful forelimbs to wrestle down small trees and pull up roots and tubers.

Both run only on their hind limbs; this is their main defence against predators. The young are leaner and longer-legged, and therefore quicker. However, the lesser *Camptosaurus* is a main menu item to just about every medium and large predator in the Morrison, while even small Coelurosaurs will take the young. The giant type is a difficult catch especially with its thumb spike and power.

For the lesser *Camptosaurus*, safety in numbers is also a useful defence. They not only travel in herds but also nest communally during the wet season out in the Foredeep, the adults protecting the breeding site from all comers. The young spend some time in the nest where they are fed by both parents. Once they are big enough, the young form huge crèches protected by the adults until large enough to leave the parental heard and form their own group; males stay in bachelor herds until they reach breeding age, when they will try to join herds with sexually mature females.

Both species are widely distributed, although the lesser type prefers more open environments; the giant species inhabits open woodland but herds also frequent gallery and riverine forests. The females of both types also change colour during the seasons, adopting more greenish camouflage during the wet season; the males of the lesser *Camptosaurus* are black with white faces, while the giant males are a more chocolate brown.

A number of small Ornithopods frequent the Morrison. *Dryosaurus* fulfils the ecological role of the gazelle, small, nimble and often in the company of larger herbivores. Its long hind limbs and tail, plus light build, make it one of the fastest animals in the Morrison. It puts its speed to good use out on the open spaces of the Foredeep, where it browses out on the fern prairies. Small herds of these 8–12ft-long runners are a frequent site out on the plains.

Less obvious are the Nanosaurs, such as *Nanosaurus*, *Drinker* and *Othnielosaurus*. These are, as the name suggests, the smallest dinosaurs of the Morrison. Some, such as *Nanosaurus*, are rarely seen, inhabiting as they do the deep forests and dense woodlands of the Front Range foothills and lowlands. Others, however, are found out on the Foredeep but remain hidden from sight because they are burrowers. They live in small family groups in dens they dig out. They nest and raise their young beneath the ground, and although generally herbivores, they are quite happy to supplement their diets with small amphibians, eggs, insects, worms and other invertebrates.

CONCLUSION

Perhaps second only to Dinosaur Park in the richness of its wildlife, the Morrison also presents the spectacle of some of the largest and greatest animals ever to have walked the Earth. It also offers the opportunity to hunt three exceptional predators in a varied environment, its wide, open spaces making it the ultimate in walking safaris!

CARRION

(Excerpt from Past Tense *by Jason Hoelzemann. Used with permission)*

I have never been comfortable with heights but I could not help but sit at the edge of the Victor's cabin, my feet hanging in the air, as the Pink Team lifted us to the campsite.

We overflew a flock of white Rhamphorhynchoids, snowy little kites streaming long ribbon-like tails tipped with a diamond. They stood out bright against the endless plains of the fern prairie, now turned to a sea of green by the new rain.

Watercourses spidered out across the plains like the pewter-coloured veins and arteries of the landscape. Rushes rippled in the breeze.

The wind from the jet wash blew over us. It was the first time I had been cool since I had arrived in the Jurassic. I enjoyed it while I could because the Pink Team was starting its descent.

Miller [the pilot] radioed, 'Drones have spotted a Theropod, seven klicks north-east.'

Alexi turned to me and raised his eyebrows. He was lit up by the morning sun and frowned when he spoke.

'Can we go straight there?'

'Sure,' said the pilot. 'We can drop you as close as you want then dump your supplies at the camp.'

Alexi leant back so he could see into the cockpit. 'Can we see a download from the drone?'

Miller linked in to our pads. The image was clean and clear, and showed a *Ceratosaurus* feeding on a dead Apatosaur.

We studied the picture.

'Is it alone?' Alexi asked the pilot. After a brief pause, the

Pink Team commander in the backseat of the Osage responded.

'Red One Actual, looks like it's alone.'

On the pad, the image pulled out as the drone controller decreased magnification. The Ceratosaur was indeed by itself. It looked small and skinny. Alexi rubbed his chin thoughtfully.

'Looks like a juvenile.'

'Scavenging,' I thought out loud.

'Too small to have made a kill like that,' said Alexi. 'Still looks pretty fresh and the body's hardly been touched.'

This was good. It meant other predators would soon be attracted. Even with so many herbivores, so many potential walking meals, passing through, scavenging was still easier, still less dangerous than killing.

We smiled at each other. 'Let's get down there then,' I said.

Alexi switched screens to the map display. He pointed to open woodland just to the south of the dead Sauropod.

'Can you put us down about two klicks to the south of the kill?' he asked Miller.

The pilot paused for a second. 'Yep, we can do that.'

From the cockpit came the crackle of comms chatter. Seconds later, Miller called, 'Hold tight.'

We gripped the cabin's open doorway. There was the sudden stomach-lurching rollercoaster motion of the tilt-rotor banking and we both lurched forward so we were looking straight down at the ground.

'We'll be at the LZ in ten minutes,' called Miller.

'Copy that,' radioed Alexi.

Once the tilt-rotor straightened out, he nodded his head into the cabin. 'Let's get ready.'

I gingerly clambered inside and made it to the canvas seat where my gear was stowed. I unzipped the case for my shotgun and slung the weapon across my chest. Alexi did the same but left the Ruger in its cover. He laid it on his lap.

'Don't worry about the ghillie suits yet,' he said. 'Let's wait until we get set up.'

I nodded. 'We should probably find a place to stow the Bergens before we head off to the site.'

'Is the Ceratosaur still there?' Alexi asked the pilot. His Russian accent came out thick.

'Yep,' Miller called back. Then, rather ominously, he asked, 'Can you get up here?'

We steadied ourselves as we staggered into the cockpit. It was not easy carrying heavy weapons, no matter how light they were supposed to be.

While Sarah [the co-pilot] flew the Victor, the pilot swivelled in his chair.

'I don't like it,' he said, anxiously.

'Like what?' I asked, a little incredulous.

'Carrion like that will draw in a lot of predators. I'm going to bring in a second drone, double the overwatch while you're on the ground. It's just a precaution.'

'Two minutes,' called Sarah.

The pilot flashed an 'OK' signal then turned back to us. 'I'm putting one of the tankers on alert five, just in case we need to stay out longer, but, again, that's just a precaution.'

He nodded towards the cabin. 'You guys better get prepped for dust-off.'

The Victor made a slow, descending turn to the left. As we headed back into the cabin, I had to steady myself and try not to think about airsickness.

Once seated, Alexi rhythmically tapped the cabin floor with his foot, perhaps from excitement, perhaps from trepidation. He stroked the rifle that was now back in his lap as though calming a swaddled child.

Through the cabin's open door, I watched the engine nacelles swivel to the vertical position. The downwash began kicking up dead leaves and detritus, but the recent rain had dampened down the dust.

There was a thump as the Victor touched down and sank into its wheel wells. Immediately, Freely [the crew chief] called, 'Let's go!'

We jumped down and he tossed us our Bergens then waved.

'Good to go?' asked Miller over the comms. He was watching us from the cockpit.

I gave him an OK signal. He flicked a salute at us then I heard the mounting roar of the engines powering up.

We dropped to one knee and ducked away from the blasting downwash as the tilt-rotor rose. Debris swirled around us and I tugged down my goggles. I looked up in time to see the Victor transit to horizontal flight and curve up and away. The Osage fell in behind it and the two headed up, their engines' noses fading into the distance.

And, once more, we were alone in the Jurassic.

Natural sounds replaced the thunder of engines. Crickets chirped. There was the buzz of flies and other animal noises that I didn't recognize, while the breeze sighed amongst the conifers and maidenhairs around us. The trees looked heavily pruned, their branches denuded as high as the largest Sauropod could reach.

The ground that had looked so lush and green from on high was actually churned, cratered with hundreds of footprints that had flattened the ferns and ground pines into a carpet of flattened leaves and stalks. Much of the new growth had been grazed to nothing but nubbins, but everywhere was the sure sign that many dinosaurs had passed this way: dung. Piles of it were everywhere, pats and spheres and Sauropod apples. Flies swarmed over them and were a draw for our first dinosaur of the day, a little, skipping *Drinker* or similar. With the Pink Team gone, little heads appeared from their underground burrows but they remained agitated and only one or two braved the open to snap at the insects and pick at the dung for seeds and shoots.

I took a compass heading and pointed north with the blade of my hand. Alexi nodded. There would be no more talking unless we had to.

I actually didn't need the compass. A spiralling cyclone of pterosaurs marked the site of the dead Apatosaur I no longer thought of as a 'kill'. Looking at the ground around me, and thinking about the freshness of the cadaver, it was much more likely that this was a sickly individual that had fallen behind its herd and died only a short while ago.

It was morning but already hot. I didn't miss the weight of the ghillie suit; however I missed its air conditioning. I trailed behind Alexi, regularly walking backwards to check behind us, the shotgun cradled in my arms, fingers on the trigger guard.

There were larger animals ahead. A heat haze shimmering off the prairie made it hard to identify them but they were moving on all fours, or so it seemed, but we exercised caution and slowed. We both dropped to one knee and pulled out binoculars from our coveralls.

It didn't take a second to identify the dinosaurs ahead. They were Camptosaurs, a bachelor herd of seven young males, each with the same cream-coloured head of a mature adult but a velvet chocolate-brown body rather than the deep black of a breeding-age male. They were not fully grown, perhaps 10–15ft long, and still rather skinny. They had narrow, beaked, sheep-like heads, but with a brow ridge over their eyes that made them look angry. At their age, safety was in numbers; too young to breed, too old to stay with the females, they were driven out by the older males and formed little bands, but it was a dangerous time for the youngsters. Accordingly, they often associated with a bigger, better-armed and more dangerous species, *Stegosaurus*, and this was just such an occasion.

Two of the giant plated dinosaurs swaggered from out amongst the conifers, thagomizers swinging back and forth. They were males, the towering plates blazing with colour in the morning sun and their chainmail wattles glistened. And they were massive, 20ft long and 3 tons, but with small heads not unlike those of the Camptosaurs, just a little more elongated. One of them flexed its forelimbs and pushed up, bear-like and clumsy, so that it could crop the crown of a tree fern. It couldn't stand fully upright but pivoted diagonally on its hips, its tail dropping to the ground in support. Lithe little Dryosaurs skipped in to snap up fronds that helicoptered down. The mane of thin bristles on their backs were an iridescent emerald and bright blue that shone as they darted around the thunderous Stegosaurs.

The Camptosaurs grazed low on all fours, but even with the presence of the Stegosaurs, one was always standing up on his hind legs, watching, only dropping to all fours when another male stood, usually with a mouth bedecked with fern fronds.

I snapped some images of the assemblage before we moved on. The circling pterosaurs seemed to leave the herbivores untroubled, which we took as a good sign as we passed among them, the highest point of the Stegosaurs' tallest plates way above our heads.

I checked in with the Pink Team.

'Is the Ceratosaur still there, over?'

The gunship commander came back to me. 'Copy that. Other than him, picture is clear.'

Picture clear. No other predators in the vicinity.

We already had our Allosaur. We *really* wanted a *Torvosaurus*.

Alexi knelt once to study the map display. With a finger, he circled a copse of trees about 100 yards to the south-east of the dead Sauropod.

'Should take about 20 minutes to get there,' I said.

Alexi slipped the Ruger from its case and slung the elephant gun over his shoulder. The Bergen straps dug into my shoulder and the rebreather mask itched as we stalked through heavily grazed prairie. I batted flies from my eyes.

Dryosaurs stopped browsing to watch us pass. The nearest trotted away, long tails curved out behind them, manes swishing.

We came up on the Ceratosaur through the thinning woods. The ground was pockmarked with crisscrossing streams of footprints and the air was full of insects swarming around piles of dung.

The Ceratosaur was a jittery young male, still without adult colours, markings still yet to fully develop and clumps of baby down matted to him here and there. He was eating fast, tearing off chunks of meat and bolting them down, blood flying. Pterosaurs and long-legged running crocs swarmed about him, the fliers knuckling about like bats coloured as seagulls. The crocs were like armoured cats with long tails and short snouts. They were perhaps *Fruitachampsa*, from the small head and size – little more than 3ft. They squabbled with each other over bloody scraps or with the pterosaurs, who struck back with their sharp beaks. Occasionally the Ceratosaur would snap at them with his gore-covered jaws and the scavengers would scatter, but only briefly; the Sphenosuchians looking even more like naked cats as they came creeping back.

There were still no other large carnivores to be seen and his belly was swollen but the Ceratosaur still ate urgently. Young and anxious, and no doubt an inexperienced hunter, he no doubt fed whenever he could, perhaps never sure when he would get the chance again.

The rebreathers were at 85 per cent efficiency when we headed towards the stand of *Araucarians*. Ever cautious, Alexi paused and ran his binoculars over the copse, studying the shadows for the slightest movement that could mark the presence of a predator. Yet there was nothing but the wind in the trees and he finally waved us on.

Alexi needed a raised position to overlook the site. He found the upended roots of a long-dead tree that gave him what he needed, once he had cleared away moss and a few dried-out ferns. He could kneel with the Ruger resting on the crumbling bark and we ranged the rifle. The wind was light and there was little haze so we had excellent visibility.

I checked in with the Pink Team, which was refuelling in flight. The drones were on overwatch and all was quiet so we settled and had breakfast while enjoying the spectacle of life in the Jurassic.

While we ate our MREs and drank from our waterpacks, the young *Ceratosaurus* finally seemed to have eaten his fill. He hissed and roared at the scavengers, sending the bandy-legged crocs scuttling and the pterosaurs flapping skyward. But he seemed to get bored of that quickly and went back to toothing the meat of the Sauropod's soft belly but without enthusiasm.

He wandered a few steps from the carcass and settled onto his belly then rolled on to his side, watching sleepily while the Sphenosuchians and pterosaurs mobbed the body.

Despite the shade, the temperature climbed in the copse as the sun did the same overhead. Rays of light streamed through the Araucarians' cloud-shaped canopies, spotlighting insects dancing in the air like moots before my eyes. I pulled on my insect hood to try to fend off the cloud of biting insects that circled my head. A tuatara-like lizard darted in and snapped one up and scuttled off, wings protruding from either side of his mouth.

Sweat beaded on my forehead then ran down my face. Alexi had leant back into the cradle that the tree roots formed around him and snoozed. I cleared the sweat from around the eyepieces of my binoculars and studied the Ceratosaur. He seemed sound asleep. A small male Coelurosaur had joined the running crocs to scavenge, protofeathers ruffled as he squabbled noisily with the nimble Sphenosuchians.

The radio clicked.

'Jurassic, this is Pink One Actual, how copy?' It was the Pink Team commander, in the backseat of the gunship. Alexi opened his eyes.

'Pink One Actual, this is Jurassic. Copy loud and clear.'

'Jurassic, drone picked up a pack of Allosaurs rendezvousing on your position from the north-east, how copy?'

'I copy, Pink One Actual.'

'Be advised we count three adults and a number of young.'

'Roger, Pink One, we'll take that under advisement.'

I turned to Alexi. These were not potential targets for us. The rifle was still at rest on the tree but he did pick up the shotgun and rest it in his lap.

'They're here for the Sauropod,' I said.

He just nodded and lifted his binoculars.

As if on cue, the Ceratosaur's head snapped up and he turned to the north-east. He rolled on to his belly and, swollen with meat, struggled upright. His jaws swung open and he let out a long hiss, raising up a cloud of flies that had settled to feed on the blood covering his muzzle. Then, he turned and headed south.

The running crocs, the pterosaurs and the Coelurosaur seemed unconcerned.

Alexi pulled his camera and stood. We leant around the tree roots to look to the north-east, and there they were – a crèche of Allosaurs.

The three adults were all females herding a gaggle of fluffy chicks. They had probably all nested and raised their young together. The chicks were noisy and nervous, and seemed to move as one big, downy mass.

'Cute,' said Alexi and snapped photos.

In complete contrast to the young Ceratosaur the adult Allosaurs had stomachs that were clearly empty. They looked bowed in and their ribs stood out under their dull hides. They had probably not eaten a full meal since the young had hatched, most of the prey going to the chicks, but now, before them, lay a veritable banquet. The leading female began to trot towards the carcass and gave a roar that startled the chicks, who dropped to the ground as they did sometimes when their mothers became nervous or to hide from predators.

When the females didn't stop, the gaggle of chicks snaked along to catch them up and only slowed once they were in the shadow of their mothers, but they had to trot just to keep up. Their parents were striding quickly towards the dead Sauropod (which I had identified as a sub-adult *Apatosaurus*) torn between motherhood and hunger.

When the first female reached the kill, the scavengers scattered, although many didn't go too far, pausing to wait with reptilian patience or to effortlessly ride the thermals so that their shadows circled the carcass below, looking more like rays beneath a murky ocean's surface.

Despite the presence of their young, the primary concern of the females seemed to be to slacken their own hunger first. Biologically, this made sense. How could they defend their young in a weakened state? Even from where we were hidden we could hear the sound of meat being rent apart and the clack of jaws. The blood and flesh seemed to agitate the females and they snapped and hissed at each other, which made the anxious chicks even more fearful. They piped and squawked at their unhearing mother, and huddled together for safety.

However, one of the mothers finally overcame her own hunger and dropped a ravaged ribbon of meat amongst the young. The chicks went from fear to greed in a split second and immediately set about the bloody provender. A pecking order soon became clear. Larger chicks bullied away the smaller ones and noisily fought one another or engaged in tugs of war over rashers of Sauropod flesh. Their down was soon matted with blood.

I was soon concerned about filling up my camera's hard drive! Such behavioural interactions were vital science and I was proud to be able to contribute to our greater understanding of these magnificent predators.

Meanwhile, Alexi's Ruger sat forlornly on the tree.

The mothers' guts filled at a staggering rate, the females gaping their jaws obscenely wide and jerking their heads back to slice away the flesh with their batteries of serrated teeth, their thick neck muscles bunching, sometimes aided by a taloned foot planted against the carcass to provide leverage.

It seemed for every two mouthfuls they took, the third would go to the young so that even the smallest was able to dine well, especially once the bigger chicks had eaten their fill. Some were so ravenous they ate until they vomited then carried on eating! Even the vomit was not wasted; the little running crocs, apparently untroubled by the carrion's condition, darted in to snap it up, trotting away triumphantly, although one had to give up its loot after it was chased down by the Coelurosaur. After a brief pursuit, the Sphenosuchian dropped the meat and scampered away while the little dinosaur bolted down its prize.

It was no more than 30 minutes after the Allosaurs had arrived that the radio once again buzzed in my earpiece.

'Jurassic, Front Range. Be advised, Torvosaurs coming up on you from the south-east.'

Alexi and I both straightened.

'Copy, Front Range.'

I couldn't believe our luck.

Alexi knelt and shouldered the Ruger, checking it over.

'Be advised, Jurassic, it's a mother and young.'

Alexi cursed loudly.

'Front Range, Pink One Actual, it's actually a pair.'

Alexi sighed and lowered the rifle. These Torvosaurs would be off limits. Still, it would hopefully provide us with a front row seat to a potentially interesting encounter between two of the Morrison's major predator species. Different habitats and different ecological niches meant they rarely cross paths so this was indeed a wonderful opportunity.

Even if we never fired a shot.

With a northerly breeze, the Allosaurs didn't need to see trouble coming. The three adults turned as one and sniffed sharply. The largest rumbled out a short, concise growl and the chicks, dozing with full bellies, immediately clustered around the legs of the nearest female. They didn't know what we knew, didn't know exactly what was coming, but even with the chicks they seemed unwilling to abandon the carcass. They had eaten plenty, even if not their fill, and wouldn't need to eat again for days, but they had many little, greedy mouths to feed and if they could hang on to it, the carcass would be an ideal short-term answer to their needs.

The females became agitated. They sniffed and roared, while pacing back and forth, the gaggle of chicks rushing back and forth, trying to keep up with their anxious mothers. And while the Allosaurs were distracted, the running crocs and pterosaurs seized their chance, returning surreptitiously to feed.

'There,' said Alexi. His binoculars were raised and he pointed south.

The Torvosaurs were indeed impressive. We both reached for our cameras.

The female was leading. She was bigger than the male and her spotted and dappled hide, better suited for their more regular forest and woodland home, made her very striking out on the sparse fern prairie. The male trailed, his bright suite of colourful display markings on his huge head almost looking like the fiery go-faster decals of a drag racer. Around him, his brood of chicks, older-looking than those of the Allosaurs, taller and more elegant, but their down ragged with age. They were also fewer in numbers, which was, no doubt, as much attributable to the rate of attrition as to the Torvosaurs' smaller clutch sizes.

They did not make a bold approach, choosing instead to slow and circle off to the right, which put them on a collision course with us. It was a heart-stopping moment as they came striding towards us, even the young, legs more stately than gangly, having the elegant tread of a secretary bird.

Alexi lifted the Ruger off the tree and gestured with his head that we move behind the cover of the tree roots. I didn't need telling twice and while I felt no compulsion to take the safety off the shotgun, my thumb wasn't a million miles from it. I took deep calming breaths as the Torvosaur family began to tower over us and the female was close enough to us that when she finally replied to the roarings of the Allosaurs, it shook needles from the *Araucarians* and dust from their bark. It was one of those sounds you didn't just hear but felt and I shuddered with the thrill of it.

Beside me, Alexi calmly took photo after photo. The Pink Team must have been watching the footage from our head cams but kept silent. I imagined the crew of the Victor clustered around the MFDs [multi-function displays] and felt a strange sense of satisfaction. This was, after all, why we had come to the Jurassic.

The encounter turned into something of a Mexican standoff. Both parties wanted the carcass but with chicks to tend, neither side seemed willing to get into a fight, not even the usually verbose and aggressive Allosaurs. If it was to be war, the sides were roughly balanced; the Allosaurs were a little smaller and less robust than the Torvosaurs, but there were three of them and they were more aggressive.

The contest, instead, became a roaring one, both predators thundering away at each other so loudly it made me squint and cover my ears. I could hear the crackle of feedback on our mikes.

This went on for a quarter of an hour and it was finally the Allosaurs who blinked, one of the females leading the chicks away to the north-west while the other two made a great show of noise and posturing, as though reminding the Torvosaurs that this was not a retreat but a withdrawal. Then, they too turned about and departed.

Calm followed. The scavengers that had been scattered by the confrontation came slinking back, including now a kind of long-legged, well-armoured Sphenosuchian croc of a type we had not seen before, later identified as *Macelognathus*. It was the biggest type of these running crocodiles and was certainly impressive, terrorizing the smaller types.

The Torvosaurs set about the carcass, the parents working one of the forelimbs, ripping at it until it came away from the Sauropod's body with a crack I usually associated more with felling trees than disintegrating bone.

The leg was for the chicks, who fed upon it noisily, squabbling and fighting, while the parents dined on the offal and guts, the male's bright colours swallowed by a stew of semi-digested plant matter from the Apatosaur's split-open stomach.

We enjoyed the sights and sounds for a while, taking pictures and shooting film, until finally Alexi turned to me.

'What say we head back and get the camp set up?' he asked.

I shrugged. 'Sure.'

I checked in with the Pink Team. 'We're looking to return to the campsite and get set up.'

'Do you want a pick-up?' Miller asked.

I turned to Alexi, who was packing up his Ruger. 'Let's walk.'

'Really?' I said. The sun was climbing high and the temperature was soaring with it.

Alexi shrugged. 'We can be back in time for lunch. Besides, the exercise will do us good.' I took this to mean this would really be our first chance to do a real walking safari in the Morrison. So far, it had been mainly short trips to hides and rides in the Victor. We hadn't had any real opportunities to 'experience' the Jurassic.

We checked the map. The ground was pretty open with no deep forest to contend with. A steady walk, the trip would take little more than 45 minutes.

'Pink Zero One, Jurassic,' I called. 'We'll walk, if you don't mind.'

'Standby,' called Miller.

A minute or two passed then the comms clicked. 'Copy, Jurassic. We'll cover you as far as the camp, then we'll head back to the FOB.'

'Copy, Pink Zero One. Flamingo out.'

Miller clicked the receiver twice to acknowledge receipt of my message.

Alexi and I checked the shotguns, took a drink then shouldered our Bergens and set off.

We stayed in the shadows as we left the Araucarian stand,

not really wanting to attract the attention of the Torvosaurs but, their bellies already swollen, we needn't have worried.

We still had plenty of time on the rebreathers although the strenuous exercise of walking in the late Morrison morning with full packs reminded me to keep an eye on mine and I reminded Alexi to do the same.

'Stop fussing,' he said and smiled. The Ruger was slung across the top of his Bergen.

Our trail took us southwards and we soon found ourselves enjoying the company of mixed herds of Camptosaurs, Dryosaurs and Othnielosaurs. Pterosaurs sat, wings folded, on the backs of the bigger Camptosaurs, the biggest we'd seen, belonging to an eland-sized species travelling in a mixed herd of females and a single male, and their shaggy young. They were joined by the smaller type, the females in their wet season greens, their stripped markings narrower than the bigger type. Gaggles of the little Dryosaurs and even littler Othnielosaurs weaved their way through the bigger Ornithopods.

Despite our being roughly the size of a Coelurosaur and just as bipedal, the Camptosaurs seemed unconcerned by our presence and we found we could get quite close to them before they turned jittery and shied away, honking and braying, the pterosaurs flapping up and away in a whistle of soft leathery wings but then gliding back down to settle once more on their mobile roost who quickly returned to grazing the ferns. Around them the Dryosaurs and Othnielosaurs scrabbled for roots and tubers, the latter not afraid to snap up any insects, larvae, grubs or worms that their excavations uncovered.

The herds were heading roughly in our direction so we fell in with them. The big Camptosaurs stirred up other creatures, lizards darting out from under their stately tread, Nanosaurs ducking back into their burrows when the shadows of the Ornithopods passed.

We felt safe, sure that the ever-watchful eyes and noses of those on guard duty would warn us of trouble. Still, it came as no surprise when I got a call from the Pink Team.

'Flamingo, you're a little too deep in that herd and we keep losing you in the trees.'

The gunship was right. The occasional conifer had given way to thicker woodland and increasing underbrush. There were dense stands of cycads and tree ferns, copses of *Araucarians* and towering conifers.

'Copy,' I called.

'Can you bear west, it's a little more open there, little less populated.'

Alexi cut in. 'Pink One Zero, you worry too much.'

I took a compass reading and indicated with my hand where we were heading. For all his bravado, Alexi still nodded and tacked to his right. He even picked up the pace.

It was about then that I noticed the wounded *Dryosaurus*. It was a male, his usually upright back mane hung limp to one side, the colours waning. His head and tail were hung low and the wound on his flank I took to be crusted in dried blood was actually black with flies. When his ribs twitched, the flies burst into the air and I saw that the wound was fresh, a long gash bright with blood.

'Alexi,' I called and pointed.

He turned and looked.

'Could be something, could be nothing,' he said and walked on.

I was still standing watching the Dryosaur when suddenly everything felt wrong. Around me, several of the Camptosaurs stopped browsing and rose on to their back legs. They looked about and the largest male gave a warning honk. Around me others began trotting past on their hind limbs, not galloping but agitated. Alexi either didn't see or didn't care. He kept on striding away from me.

I called his name.

He turned as Dryosaurs and Othnielosaurs suddenly bolted, some kangarooing in high jumps, their manes high, as they gave sharp calls. They were scared.

The Camptosaur chicks clustered about the female guards, some rising to look about.

Then, they all turned in one direction, to the south, where Alexi had his shotgun in his hands. Camptosaurs thudded past and although I was no more than 30ft from him, I kept losing sight of him.

'Jason,' he cried and over the Pink Team channel I heard Miller calling, 'Guns, guns, guns!'

'What is it?' I cried.

But already the Camptosaurs were slowing and settling. *Nothing big*, I thought, *or they'd be stampeding*. But the smaller Ornithopods were still anxious, some fleeing, others freezing, jogging a few steps then freezing again, looking south.

I started to run towards Alexi, calling his name. It would have taken just seconds to cover the distance but that was all the time it took for the Coelurosaur to come charging out from behind a herd of the giant Camptosaurs. It was as long and lean as one of the Dryosaurs and it took me a second to realize what I was seeing. There was a heart-stopping moment when I thought it was going for Alexi but then the wounded Dryosaur was there and the Coelurosaur bore down on it.

It jinked hard to the right and ran straight at Alexi.

I called his name once more as he brought the shotgun up to his shoulder and fired.

Even a baton round would have deterred the Coelurosaur but the round went wide. I could hear calm voices on the comms saying there was trouble and they were right.

Maybe it was something in the way Alexi moved that made

the predator suddenly change his focus. Maybe it was his strange shape. Maybe it made him look wounded or slow, but whatever it was, it – a male *Tanycolagreus* they told me later, long after I was past caring – charged.

Alexi fired off another round that hit the Coelurosaur in the shoulder. It screamed but its jaws struck him in the face at the same moment as he fired again, uselessly, into the air.

The predator swung its long neck and short head to one side, powerful enough to lift Alexi off his feet. He was swung to the ground and the Coelurosaur grabbed him by the shoulders.

Some part of me knew I only had one shot. The gunship might well have been on its way, but this predator was too small for its cannon and it was now 'danger close' – a ludicrous term under the circumstances.

It was down to me. I dropped to one knee and focused down the iron sights. Alexi wasn't calling my name any more. There was just a strange whining and gurgling. I waited for the space between heartbeats, my finger on the trigger, but the Coelurosaur was thrashing about and it wasn't like I was shooting targets, even like shooting a deer. It was like tracking a fast-flying mallard.

Finally, it stopped moving.

I lined up on its armpit, the angle where its shoulder blade met its humerus.

I fired.

It was a perfect shot. The solid slug wouldn't have been stopped by the Coelurosaur's fragile ribs and it probably blew its heart to pieces.

The lean, beautiful predator was knocked off its feet and into the dirt. It twitched briefly then nothing.

Alexi, I realized, was alive and continued to struggle. I ran to him as I heard the sound of rotorblades overhead.

I was calling his name but he didn't recognize me. Even if he did, there was nothing he could say. He had no throat to say it with. His blood was soaking into the earth and already flies were landing on it. I did the usual that people do under similar circumstances – similar in terms of dying, that is, not dying after having your throat ripped out by a dinosaur – there was nothing usual in that. I told him help was coming, that he'd be fine, he'd be doing his favourite things soon enough, but the blood was like a garden sprinkler, spurting out and pooling. There was, I realized, a part of the Jurassic that would be forever Alexi.

The wounded Dryosaur watched me briefly as I tried to apply pressure to Alexi's neck, but already, the fountain had become a dribble and his eyes had rolled over white. I still see those dead white eyes sometimes.

This is your bloody fault, I thought at the Dryosaur but if he heard he seemed untroubled, trotting away to make room for the landing Victor, too little and way too late.

How the Tanycolagreus went unnoticed was later attributed to the inexperience of the drone operator at the Front Range FOB; he failed to recognize the shift in behaviour amongst the Camptosaurs and their sudden anxiety; he also failed to identify the Coelurosaurs. However he was exonerated by MHC® after simulation of the incident showed that even experienced operators had a hard time picking out the Tanycolagreus from larger number of herbivores and the thick woodland.

Alexi Feifer's family unsuccessfully sued MHC® for misconduct and breach of contract. Feifer's remains were buried in his native Kiev.

Jason Hoelzemann is still CEO of a very successful cyber security firm in Singapore. He returned to the Jurassic once more, this time as the shooter, before writing a very successful book of his experiences. He has also contributed funds to science-based expeditions to the Mesozoic.

THE BAHARIYA FORMATION

Period: Late Cretaceous
Age: Cenomanian stage (98–93 mya)
Present location: North Africa
Reserve size: approx 2,100 square miles (a little smaller than Everglades National Park)

CONDITIONS

By about 100 mya, the supercontinents had begun to break up and the landmasses began to resemble their current state. Africa was further south than where it lies currently, largely below the equator. The Bahariya is situated in what is now Egypt but rather than desert, the area was a vast coastal delta situated on the north-eastern edge of Africa as part of the southern coastline of the Tethys Sea. Global temperatures remained high, although carbon dioxide levels were lower than their Triassic and Jurassic highs; approximately four times higher than current pre-industrial levels. Accordingly, conditions remained distinctly tropical, with distinct wet and dry seasons, the former lasting some seven months. Temperatures averaged 18°C (65°F); during the dry season, temperatures swelled to 32.2–40.5°C (09–105°F). This is lower than temperatures in the continent's interior, mainly as a result of the cooling effect of the Tethys Sea.

GEOGRAPHY AND ENVIRONMENT

The Bahariya Reserve is located close to the Tethys coast. Its initial appearance is not unlike that of the Florida Everglades or Sundarban Mangroves. It is fed by a large number of rivers, streams and creeks heading in a generally north–south direction.

The south of the reserve is largely dense forest broken up by freshwater drainage channels and winding rivers that break the landscape up into hammocks. The hammocks are covered pines, conifers, laurels, plane trees, sapindales of many kinds, and kauri trees. The creeks and bayous are lined with old growth cypress, pond apples and stands of horsetails, cattails and scouring reeds.

The hammocks are often surrounded by pine flatwood wetlands and meadows of fern and palmetto. The hammocks and flatwoods are the habitat of Iguanodonts (as yet undescribed officially); the most common is similar to *Lurdusaurus* and a sail-backed type akin to *Ouranosaurus*, both from earlier in the Cretaceous. Also present in large numbers is the small Sauropod, *Aegyptosaurus*. These are prey for the giant Theropod, *Carcharodontosaurus*.

Further north, the rivers and their tributaries break up still further in a network of tidal creeks slowly running through sloughs and mudflats that are largely flooded during the wet season. The erosion created limestone marls that combine with bacteria, algae, fungi and detritus to form a thick sludge-like coating called periphyton. This covers roots, clings to rushes and horsetails, and forms dense mats that provide a food resource to small fish and invertebrates. The shallow waters surround hundreds of small islands covered in thickets and forests or cypress domes that have their own microclimates. Larger ones can also have freshwater 'croc holes'. These are burrows dug by large crocodilians such as *Aegyptosuchus* to escape the worst of the dry season. These freshwater pools provide vital homes for fish, amphibians, birds and pterosaurs, where they see out the year.

Further north, the freshwater slough gives way to brackish water environments and the cypress is replaced by mangroves; these form a frontier with the ocean. The mangroves cover many of the small islands or rise in clumps along the tidal flats that form the frontier with the sea. These islands provide nesting sites for pterosaur colonies while the submerged root systems are nurseries for many fish and marine reptiles that come inshore to breed. These nurseries attract various predators, including *Spinosaurus*, various species of shark and predatory marine reptiles, particularly small to medium-sized Pliosaurs.

There are also large swathes of oyster banks along the tideline, which provide food for the Azhdarchid pterosaur, *Alanqa* and the terrestrial crocodile, *Libycosuchus*.

The wet season sees Bahariya produce high levels of rainfall; this, combined with storm surge coming in from coastal waters, raises water levels across the reserve, presenting the threat of flooding that inundates the sloughs and wetlands. Many of the meadows to the south are flooded. The coastline is also lashed by frequent tropical storms coming in off the Tethys Sea; hurricane-force winds and storm surges can seriously damage the forest coverings of smaller hammocks and mangrove islands.

However, the wet season is when much of the Bahariya's wildlife breeds, making use of the growth spurred on by the increased availability of water and the resulting effect this has on the ecosystem. The dry season sees these water levels dropping considerably and many of the small watercourses desiccating to cracked mud.

The Bahariya is unique amongst the MHC® reserves in that it requires special equipment. While rebreathers remain a necessity, the riverine conditions mean that walking is often difficult to impossible. Accordingly, hunting parties are equipped with electrically powered skiffs or skimmers, small two-person boats with very shallow drafts that enable the vessel to negotiate the wetlands, flatwoods and even the flattened fern and palmetto meadows. They are also quite capable coastal vessels and stable gun platforms.

LICENSED TARGETS

You are licensed to hunt the following species in the Bahariya:

SPINOSAURUS

Length: 50ft
Weight: 20 tons
One of the true giants in the pantheon of large Theropods, *Spinosaurus* is also very unusual in its physical form, being one of the few true dinosaurs adapted for a life in water. While the figures above are general for its size, larger individuals are suspected.

In appearance, it's not a million miles from a sail-backed crocodile; its narrow, elongated jaws also feature a quite crocodilian kink and tooth plan, with large teeth restricted to the tip of the snout, where they (and the jaws) interlock. The nostrils are unusual in being quite far back, allowing the snaring teeth to be held below the water's surface. A small crest is also present between the eyes, set far back and raised high in the skull. All these features seem related to aquatic adaptations and while its function does not pertain to any kind of swimming or feeding activity, the crest reflects a similar feature seen in the very distantly related crocodile-like Phytosaurs (see the Chinle section), where males possess a distinct crest along the midline of the skull.

The limbs are also very different to those of most Theropods, with an almost quadrupedal layout. The forelimbs are large and well muscled, and sport a large hooked talon, bigger in the males; this claw is used in hunting and defence against large predators it may have cause to cross paths with, such as *Carcharodontosaurus*. Males also use them to spar during the mating season while females put them to good use discouraging males away from nests and young during the breeding season. The feet are slightly webbed.

The rear legs are unlike any other Theropods. They are surprisingly small, only a little larger than the forelimbs, so that the *Spinosaurus* body plan really is little different from that of a crocodilian. The generally reduced size of the hind limbs restricts locomotion on dry land, although it puts into shore to rest or, in the case of the females, nest.

However, the most striking feature of *Spinosaurus* is its great sail, formed from the extremely long neural spines of the animal's back vertebrae. Broadly similar to the sail of another famous (but non-dinosaurian and much earlier) predator, *Dimetrodon*, its structure is not designed for thermoregulation but, with much of its time spent in water, for display and fat storage; the stores are built up in the dry season, although the females also use their sails to store fat prior to their breeding season fast (see below).

The sails are also distinctly sexually dimorphic. Male Spinosaurs are generally smaller than the females but have proportionally larger sails that are also far more brightly marked; the males use them in colourful displays that are used in preference, where possible, to physical contests, fighting being really only a last resort and involving a clash of jaws and slashing attacks with the large claws. The males also use them to signal to females, who use their own to signal their willingness or indifference to mating, as well as warning curious males away from eggs or young.

As would be expected with such a well-adapted semi-aquatic animal, fish is a Spinosaur's primary prey. The Bahariya offers a wealth of large fish types on which to feed, including the very common *Lepidotes* and tuna-like *Paranogmius*, both of which can grow huge, the latter to over 12ft. It will also take gar, lungfish, hybodont sharks and sawfish, all of which are abundant in the waters of the Bahariya. They will also take small crocodilians, even turtles, especially the soft-backed types.

During the dry season, *Spinosaurus* is found most frequently amongst the creeks, bayous and channels of the slough and cypress wetlands, where it feeds on the large numbers of fish and aquatic vertebrates trapped by the season's receding waters.

At the start of the wet season, the Spinosaurs move out into the more open sloughs and mangrove flats. Spending so much time in water, the sail takes on its primary function, that of sexual attractor; the colours change, becoming bright and, to the females, more alluring. The females spend the latter part of the dry season fattening up; this is when Spinosaurs are most likely to be found on land, as they make their way to shrunken pools or wallows where fish have been trapped or suffocated; they will also use their massive

A *Spinosaurus* plies his way through coastal mangroves. A *Sirrocopteryx* soars overhead.

claws to dig out lungfish. Once the wet season arrives, they are able to eat well on the many fish drawn into the watershed to breed.

After mating, the females choose small hammocks or islands, usually quite isolated, on which to nest and lay their eggs. They also fast during this period.

Laying in such isolated spots keeps the nest relatively safe; the main threat comes from terrestrial crocs who also happen to be excellent swimmers, and who will put ashore on these small islands if they find an unattended nest or a distracted female.

The real threat, though, is from cannibal males, who often swim out into the watershed to hunt young and eggs. This leads to frequent battles, although the smaller males often get the worst of any conflict.

Once the young are born, they are abandoned by the female, who continues to fast until a week or so after hatching; the young stay amongst the mangrove roots or in shallow water, where they hunt insects and small fish.

The hungry females now prowl the mangrove flats or head back inland to hunt. They also threaten pterosaur colonies, coming ashore to plunder nests for eggs and chicks. They will even take adults if hungry.

Spinosaurs are very rarely social; the only time they may be seen in numbers is if they gather to feed on a mass stranding of fish or the occasional marine reptile; this is when they are also most likely to encounter other large Bahariya Theropods. However, such encounters rarely end well for the *Spinosaurus*, ironically out of their depth on land, and vulnerable to the likes of such giant predators as *Carcharodontosaurus*, who will also take young Spinosaurs, unafraid to attack them in the water.

CARCHARODONTOSAURUS

Length: 40ft
Weight: 8 tons
The terrestrial apex predator of the Bahariya, *Carcharodontosaurus* is in general appearance a typical large Theropod – long-legged and long-tailed, with a relatively stocky frame and short but powerful forelimbs, including a large claw on the first digit. The head is large, with a large lower jaw and triangular skull. Its senses are well developed, particularly smell and hearing, which are more effective in its preferred habitat: the dense forests of the Bahariya interior and the hammocks of the wetlands and swamps. It is also very comfortable in water and a capable swimmer.

Carcharodontosaurs regularly hunt in water, especially in the dry season when they will quite happily attack large fish trapped in shallow water; they'll also kill young Spinosaurs. In fact, for this apex predator, virtually nothing is off Bahariya's menu. Their primary prey is Iguanodonts and Sauropods. To hunt and kill these, *Carcharodontosaurus* employs the classic 'land shark' stratagem, ambushing from dense cover, and using its scalpel-shaped tooth pattern to make slashing wounds. This is further aided by the blade-like serrated teeth, not unlike those of the great white shark (hence the name), which are extremely adept at slicing open flesh.

Unless the prey is sufficiently small to be overwhelmed in the initial attack, the Carcharodontosaur then withdraws and lets blood loss and shock take its toll. If need be, it will stay with the prey and deliver further attacks until the victim is completely incapacitated and easily dispatched. These predations can take many hours, even days, and make for a long, lingering death for the prey, which can end up being virtually eaten alive. This method means that even the largest animal of the Bahariya, *Paralititan*, is not immune from attack.

The forelimbs are limited in mobility – they aren't even capable of scratching the animal's neck – but they are quite capable of pulling prey close to the body, where the jaws can really go to work. This is probably most effective against small prey, and in dismembering carcasses.

The wet season sees many Carcharodontosaurs moving north into the hammocks, cypress domes and sloughs of the flatlands and watershed, following the Sauropods and Iguanodonts who come to browse on the fern meadows and amongst mangroves. However, following a short and usually brutal mating season, the females remain in the denser, less well-watered forests to nest. They stay with the large clutches of eggs until they hatch, then escort the precocial young into dense cover where they abandon them.

The pups have a high mortality rate (especially from males of the same species) but grow very quickly, subsisting on insects and other invertebrates initially, but soon capable of hunting small mammals and the juveniles of other dinosaur types whose breeding seasons coincide with that of *Carcharodontosaurus*. The young are also quite capable swimmers and will take small fish, frogs and other amphibians, the long wet season making food plentiful.

The dry season sees adults moving to the more forested interior, where they stay close to permanent fresh water and the prey animals it draws to it. They also enjoy wallowing in croc pools and mud holes (these provide excellent hunting opportunities) during the heat of the day.

OPPOSITE: **The sharp end of a *Carcharodontosaurus*.**

RUGOPS

Length: 20ft
Weight: 1,600lbs
A member of the strange clade of Theropods, the Abelisaurs, *Rugops* bears many of the physical hallmarks of this family: longer than average legs and tail, short trunk and very bizarrely stunted forearms with four stubby fingers; the head is short, deep and square while the roof of the snout sports a pair of raised ridges, between which is a rough, thickened plate of bone extending across the top of the skull. The lower jaw, however, is slender and the numerous teeth small. The musculature of the jaws is such that though the bite force is not strong, they can snap together with surprising speed, a feature best suited for catching small, nimble prey.

Rugops is generally terrestrial; it is comfortable in the water, as the environment requires, but is not quite as aquatic as the likes of *Carcharodontosaurus*. It generally hunts animals smaller than itself, running down small or juvenile dinosaurs, terrestrial crocodiles and turtles. A favourite tactic is to ambush pterosaurs, seizing them before they can get airborne. The primary offensive weapon are the jaws, despite their seemingly reduced size; the peculiarly atrophied forearms are more or less useless in the handling of prey, and seem to serve virtually no function at all except providing a notion of stability to the male when he mounts the female during mating.

Rugops' small size gives it greater freedom of movement in the thick riverine forests, dense hammocks and cypress domes of the Bahariya that is its primary habitat. It is also, by nature, a solitary predator with large territories; however, pairs will stay together following successful courtships. The particularly thickened skull roofs of the males are used in head-banging jousts to secure mates. Such physical prowess has selectively made the males larger than the females.

The successful pair raise the young together, two parents being more likely to see off larger predators. The nest is built in the densest part of the forest that remains accessible; parents take turns to make hunting trips and bring back meat to the young after hatching. The number of eggs laid is fewer and the young less precocious. They stay in the nest longer than other Bahariya Theropods, while the nest is often chosen to be near nesting colonies of Iguanodonts or Sauropods, making prey plentiful.

On leaving the nest, the young are bigger than many juvenile dinosaurs and they will stay with their parents until a few weeks old, when they will be abandoned and the parents go their separate ways. The young *Rugops* stay in the thick forests and swamps until they are big enough to venture out into more open flatlands and sloughs. These juveniles, without established territories, will sometimes head out as far as the watershed and coastal flats, hunting fish and raiding pterosaur colonies; they are also not at all averse to scavenging (adults will also quite happily scavenge from Carcharodontosaur kills and rob smaller predators of a meal).

Once big enough, they usually return to the interior and seek to establish territories for themselves, usually with at least one female's territory overlapping it.

OTHER FAUNA

BAHARIASAURUS

Little is known of this large but rare Theropod. Not much smaller than *Carcharodontosaurus*, at 35ft long and weighing 21/2 tons, it is more gracile and seems much more at home in a terrestrial environment. As such, it is found largely in the dense jungles of the Bahariya interior, seldom venturing into the flatwoods and meadows of the wetlands, so sightings are rare.

Being lighter and more agile than its contemporaries, its main hunting strategy would appear to be high-speed ambushes on small to medium prey; its favoured prey appears to be Iguanodonts.

Little is known of social life or reproduction. It appears to be a solitary but effective hunter but little can be said on its behaviour.

SAUROPODS

Bahariya is home to two Sauropods, both members of the Titanosaur group.

Aegyptosaurus is the smaller but more common of the two. Adults reach about 50ft in length and can weigh up to 5 tons; like many Titanosaurs, they are armoured, with backs and flanks covered in osteoderms embedded in the skin. This species is a low-browser, preferring to feed in the more open fern and palmetto prairies; it will also graze on floating ferns in shallower watercourses, where it is less vulnerable to larger predators (particularly crocodilians) that are generally restricted to deeper creeks and channels.

Herds of *Aegyptosaurus* are frequent visitors to the sloughs and hammocks closer to the Bahariya coast, especially in the wet season; they rarely venture into the cypress and mangrove flats, which would require them to travel or swim in open water and run the risk of attack of aquatic hunters; instead they are regular prey for *Carcharodontosaurus*. Moving in herds make them less susceptible to attack.

Breeding season for *Aegyptosaurus* is at the start of the wet season. It nests colonially, on sand spits or treeless islands, running the risk of storm surges and rising water levels to build nests in damp sand; the colony sites are usually in close proximity to marshland and densely vegetated hammocks. Large numbers of eggs are laid; the adults stay within the vicinity of the nests to provide protection from thieves. Hatching usually takes place at dusk which provides enough light for the young to scatter to the cover of the marshes and thick vegetation of the riverine understoreys. They grow rapidly and when large enough, groups of juveniles will form herds to venture out and join adult groups in the meadows and flatlands.

Paralititan, the second Sauropod, is a giant; it can grow up to 70ft in length and weigh over 25 tons. Unlike its

OPPOSITE: A *Rugops* paddles across a coastal channel, kicking up silt that draws the attention of a passing Pliosaur.

contemporary Sauropod, this species browses mid to high levels and in build it is somewhat convergent with the Brachiosaurs of the northern continents. It has high withers and its neck is held diagonally, making it perfectly suited to browse at height.

Small groups of these enormous herbivores migrate north and south according to the seasons. In the wet season, they move south to feed in the new growth of the lush interior forests; this is where they breed, using strategies not dissimilar to those of *Aegyptosaurus*. During the dry season, they head north and push out into the watershed, grazing in the sloughs and mangrove flatlands. The huge size of the adults makes them immune to even the largest predators and they freely travel in open water.

Paralititan is vital to the Bahariya's environmental wellbeing; far more at home in the water than many other Sauropods, its massive size is put to good use keeping channels and creeks clear of detritus and build-ups of periphyton. This keeps currents and tides moving and the water aerated, especially along the sloughs and mangrove flats.

IGUANODONTS

There are two, as yet undescribed Iguanodonts in the Bahariya, both apparently related to earlier species and not that different from them. One is a rather robust type not unlike the earlier *Lurdusaurus*; it is large, about 30ft long, with a very thickset, barrel-shaped body while the fore and hind limbs are short and roughly equal in size. As such, it is more or less a habitual quadruped, although the hands support a very large thumb spike, which is used on the few occasions the animal rises on to its hind legs; on these occasions the spike is used to deter predators or, in the case of males, rivals. Both hands and feet are rather splayed, offering support in muddy or swampy environments, which they frequent, grazing on bankside vegetation but also at home in the meadows and flatwoods. However, it is far more semi-aquatic than most Iguanodonts although it tends to avoid more brackish and seawater conditions.

Males and females exhibit a certain amount of sexual dimorphism; the male is somewhat larger and while largely black in colour, the face, limbs and tail are boldly marked. The smaller females are coloured in a 'dazzle' style of black, brown and white that breaks up their outlines in dense forest.

The females travel in small herds, usually attended by one male during the breeding season; after mating with all the sexually mature females, he joins in the colonial defence of the nest site, where all the females lay. The young are precocial but stay in the nest, where they are fed by all the adults in the herd, as part of an extended crèche.

After two to three weeks, the crèche is moved to swampland or marshes, where the young are relatively safe from Theropod predators, and bigger crocodilians. They will stay in this environment once the adults abandon them, usually moving on to the hammocks, cypress flats and fern meadows during the wet season to fatten up; here they are most vulnerable to attack by large Theropods.

The second Iguanodontid is a sailed type analogous to *Ouranosaurus*. This species is smaller than the Lurdusaur, only around 25ft in length, and more gracile, with longer limbs and neck, and a body plan not dissimilar to later Hadrosaurs (see the next chapter), a similarity borne out by the animal's more pronounced 'duckbill'. It also has a much-reduced thumb spike and therefore it may not be an Iguanodont at all but a basal Hadrosaur.

The one noticeable difference between this species and other Iguanodonts (and Hadrosaurs) is its sail; this is more pronounced than in the earlier species, with the neural spines longer over the shoulders, taking on an even stronger resemblance to a bison's hump than in *Ouranosaurus*; the impression is reinforced by the low-browsing/grazing behaviour of the animal. The males are particularly impressive due to their bright colouration; sexual selection has also resulted in the males being somewhat larger than the females.

Unlike the Lurdusaur, the sailed type is less aquatic and frequents the flatwoods and meadows, and larger hammocks. They very rarely travel into more aqueous territory, even during the dry season, when the meadows and the forests of the interior are far drier. This, however, is when the sail shows its primary function (the display purpose seems to have been an evolutionary by-product); the long wet seasons allow the Ouranosaurid to build up fat in the sail, grazing heavily on the fern and palmetto meadows. This fat sees them through the leaner times of the dry season.

The sailed Iguanodonts form herds of 10–30 individuals and nest colonially; they form the young into crèches that stay with the adults until they are old enough to independently form herds of their own. Being largely terrestrial, they are very much favoured prey of large Theropods.

PTEROSAURS

The slough, mangrove flats and the coastal zone of the Bahariya make it difficult (and dangerous) for small dinosaurs to live in safety. The many watercourses that need to be crossed make small raptors and Ornithopods very vulnerable to attack by a host of aquatic and semi-aquatic predators.

Accordingly, some of the ecological niches of the Bahariya have been taken over by pterosaurs, who can move about such a wide-open and watery environment with relative ease, flying between the hundreds of islands in search of food.

Filling the role of smaller predator is a species of *Thalassodromeus*, easily recognizable by its rugged sail-like head crest. Its toothless bill is long and powerful, while its eyes face forward, providing excellent depth of vision. Its neck is short, thick and flexible while, on the ground, the forelimbs created by the folded wings and the legs are roughly equivalent in length. All these features combine to make a flier which is almost as comfortable on the ground, where it is also an effective hunter. Strategically not dissimilar to a modern stork or a small raptorial dinosaur, *Thalassodromeus* picks its way across fern meadows, snapping up small animals, and can often be seen trailing large dinosaurs, where it will use its long bill to grab anything stirred up by the passing of the larger animals. It is also quite happy to stalk across flatlands and exposed tidal flats in search of invertebrates, lungfish and carrion. This robust and aggressive pterosaur will take on eggs, hatchlings and even juvenile dinosaurs, given the opportunity. Sexually dimorphic, the crests of the larger males are far larger and more colourful than the smaller females. Pairs nest on small mangrove islands or hammocks during the wet season, both providing for the two to three chicks (although rarely more than one survives).

The largest of the Bahariya pterosaurs is *Alanqa*, a member of the Azhdarchid family. With a wingspan of around 20ft, it stands about 6ft tall on the ground. Its beak is long and it is like most Azhdarchids in general appearance but for the raised 'bumps' approximately half way down the beak, on both sides of the upper and lower jaw. *Alanqa* has a long, stiff neck and although comfortable on the ground, it is not built to handle prey quite as kinetic as that hunted by *Thalassodromeus*. Instead, the long neck and bill, and the beak 'bumps' have evolved to harvest shellfish, especially those from the rich oyster beds of the Bahariya watershed when they are exposed at low tide. It will take other small, slow creatures that cross its path and has been known to scavenge.

Alanqa travels in small flocks and these towering, stately figures are a common sight along the Bahariya coastline as they travel across the flats in search of food. They are quite aggressive to intruders and it's not wise to approach them on foot as they are surprisingly fast runners, despite their apparently ungainly appearance. *Alanqa* also nest colonially, laying two to three eggs in simple, scraped out nests at the start of the wet season.

The Azdarchid pterosaur, Alanqa, stalks across a mudflat between the bones of dead pliosaur.

Another Bahariyan pterosaur is *Siroccopteryx*, a member of the Ornithocheirids. Distinguishing features include long spiky teeth in the tip of the jaws; the end of both jaws also sports raised semi-circular keels. The eyes are forward facing and the neck is long and flexible, while its wings are narrow and some 15ft in length. *Siroccopteryx* is ungainly on the ground, with only small hind legs, but is extremely graceful in the air, its body plan ideal for a long-distance soarer. Its diet is largely fish; it is a dip feeder, sailing low over the sea's surface and using its toothed beak to snap up prey; the beak keels provide a degree of stability (although their primary role is species recognition and sexual display), while the neck is heavily muscled to withstand the drag created when the beak punches into the water.

Not surprising for an ocean-going pterosaur, it is white in colour except for the head markings, much more accentuated in the males. They are rarely seen along the coast throughout much of the year, but come to the Bahariya coastline at the start of the wet season to mate and nest in large, noisy colonies while also taking advantage of the glut of fish that enter coastal waters to breed and use the mangrove shallows as nurseries. The nesting sites are usually on bigger mangrove islands or sand spits, as isolated as possible and therefore much safer. Thalassodromids are, however, a regular menace, pirating eggs and chicks despite the furious defence of the parents. Another threat are young Spinosaurs who will brave open water to plunder the colonies. It's wise to bear in mind that approaching one of these colonies can be a hazardous undertaking as a parent *Siroccopteryx* will dive-bomb and mob anyone foolish enough to come too close.

CROCODILIANS AND OTHER AQUATIC CREATURES

The greatest hazard to the Bahariya hunter is that of crocodilians. There are a number of types, some of which grow to incredible sizes.

An unusual croc is the freshwater *Aegisuchus*, easily recognizable by its strange flattened head and the circular lump or 'boss' behind the eyes, which are close together. Despite its unconventionally shaped head, *Aegisuchus* is still an effective ambush predator. It frequents the narrow creeks and bayous of the interior, preying on dinosaurs and large fish; its favoured stratagem is to stay on the creek bed where its flattened shape makes it hard to spot; its upward pointing eyes will then watch for any fish big enough to take on dinosaurs coming down to drink or make a crossing. This croc is one that grows to giant lengths; usually those spotted have been around 20–30ft in length but others have been seen that measured over 50ft. Some reports indicate even larger individuals.

Another giant is the as yet undescribed Sarcosuchid, apparently a descendant of the famous *Sarcosuchus* of the earlier Cretaceous. This species can grow up to 40 or more feet in length, and like its descendant, appears to be a generalist feeder. This is despite its seemingly narrow jaws that would really befit a piscivore; however, the top of the snout swells to accommodate very large teeth. Unlike types belonging to later families of crocodilians, these Sarcosuchids cannot perform the infamous 'death roll' used to dismember carcasses. Instead, the animal uses a horizontal thrashing to rip its meal into eatable chunks. This species stays out in larger watercourses and will travel out into brackish environments; it is often seen in the croc wallows at the centre of larger hammocks, cypress domes and mangrove islands.

Aegyptosuchus is another large species, growing up to 30ft. However it is, by and large, a piscivore, its appearance not very different to the modern gharial, although it's a little more robust and the jaws are not quite as narrow, proportionally. One of the most widely distributed of the Bahariya crocs, it is found anywhere that supports a population of fish. In the wet season, it travels as far out as coastal water, hunting in the mangroves and on the shoals of baitfish that come inshore to feed on the detritus washed out by storm surges. It will also take the sharks and even Polycotylids that follow the shoals in. Despite its size, it is perhaps the least dangerous of Bahariya crocs, but bigger individuals are known to supplement their diet with small dinosaurs and pterosaurs.

Libycosuchus is a dog-sized terrestrial croc, although this could be construed as something of a misnomer as it is a very effective swimmer. This Labrador-sized hunter and scavenger is very much an opportunist and seems to have replaced small dinosaurs in this role within the Bahariya ecosystem. It has broad tastes in food, eating anything from eggs, young dinosaurs and lungfish to crabs, shellfish and turtles. It will scavenge from Theropod kills and, in the wet season, has even been seen swimming out to pterosaur colonies to steal eggs and chicks, its long tail making for an effective sculling device. *Libycosuchus* nests in burrows dug into river banks or between the thick roots of cypress and mangroves.

Stomatosuchus is one of the more enigmatic of the Bahariya's crocs. Growing up to 30ft, it is unusual in that, unlike virtually every known crocodilian, it is a filter feeder, not unlike a baleen whale. Its skull is flattened along the lines of *Aegisuchus* but is lined with dozens of very small teeth. The lower jaw, however, has no teeth at all and the usual crocodilian throat pouch has expanded to resemble that of a baleen whale and is even pleated in a similar manner. *Stomatosuchus* is a very rare visitor to the Bahariya, spending much of its time in open water; however, it does come into the tidal waters during the wet season to feed on the baitfish that come inshore during this time.

Also rarely seen are Polycotylids. These marine reptiles have long dolphin-like jaws, four flippers, barrel-shaped bodies and a short tail. They are very streamlined and move with grace and speed through the water; they are also piscivores, hunting small fish. There is a freshwater species that plies the more open watercourses and rivers, but in the wet season, marine species arrive along the Bahariya coastline to give birth to live young amongst the nurseries provided by mangrove roots. These nurseries provide not only cover for the newborn but also a ready food source of small and newborn fish; this same food source is used by female Polycotylids to replenish their strength after the trauma of giving birth.

There are a number of fish that also grow to very large sizes in the water of the Bahariya. These include the voracious gar, *Atractosteus*, which can grow up to 10ft; of similar size is the lungfish, *Ceratodus*, of the same genus as the modern Queensland lungfish but much larger. The largest fish is *Paranogmius*, a tuna-like ocean-going fish that can grow up to 12ft. These are rarely seen in Bahariya waters, but occasionally one will stray into coastal waters during the wet season, seemingly in pursuit of baitfish or other prey. There are also hybodontid sharks that favour fresh and brackish water conditions, where they feed on shellfish and invertebrates such as crabs and crayfish. These can reach 7ft long. Another real giant is the bichir, *Bawitius*; growing up to 10ft long, it lives in the freshwater swamps and creeks of the interior, feeding on fish, invertebrates and juvenile crocs and dinosaurs.

Conclusion

An amazing environment for the hunter looking for something a little out of the ordinary, the Bahariya has a great deal to offer, including the chance to bag one of the most iconic movie dinosaurs, as well as a great opportunity to do some serious sports fishing!

THE BAYOU

(Blog posting by Yishan Lo. Used with permission.)

They were one week into their trip and without a kill yet, Yishan Lo and her shooter, Cheung Wing Law, when a drone spotted a number of bodies out amongst the mangrove islands at the very edge of the coast. A small herd of Paralititan *had been foraging far out amongst the mangroves and cypress domes when a tropical storm had caught them unawares. The resulting surge had flash-flooded the coast, drowning the massive Sauropods. The presence of so much carrion offered an opportunity of staking out the bodies, which were almost certain to attract large predators. The following morning, the hunting team set off...*

Mist shifted the spectrum of the morning sun to a pale orange. Swarms of biting insects danced, midges or gnats or maybe mosquitos. Cheung gunned the engine but it made little noise. Just sped us through the clouds unbitten. The trip would be long, hours by our estimate. The creek curled, switched back on itself. Oxbows and sidewinder tracks added miles to the journey as they snaked around hammocks and domes of dense forest.

The insects would have plenty more opportunities to come.

Cheung took it slow, though. The creek sides were thick with cattails and bulrushes shedding clumps of pollen. Towering horsetails so tall they looked more like bamboo. He kept the skimmer to the centre of the creek but, still, great armoured backs occasionally broke the water, throwing shockwaves that made the mats of floating, spongy ferns rise and fall in the ripples.

Fish.

Huge, dragon-scaled lungfish with pouting supermodel lips that gulped air. Bichirs, reedfish the size of the skimmer and bigger, rose alongside us and I would raise the shotgun, but a small beady eye would look us over as we sat crouched in our ghillie suits, for all the Cenomanian world like piles of dead reeds. Then, the eye would sink into the murk, leaving us untroubled.

Cheung pointed shoreward.

The riverine understorey parted and on an oxbox mudflat basked *Aegisuchus*. Jaws agape, eyes closed, lined up as symmetrically as the work of a Cretaceous logger.

Again we passed untroubled but the water seemed somehow darker. Those crocs had been longer than our boat. By a pretty major factor. But on we puttered. We passed beneath tunnels of love, a rat king's tail of roots and branches knotted into sprawling arches hung with moss. Walls of old growth cypress and pond apples, thick with gourds and ferns. Wreathes of white and pink flowers.

We floated on carpets of green that hid the dark creek water, but beneath the arches, the air was stultifying. Even with air con, we sweltered in the ghillie suits and insect hoods, and there was an almost overwhelming urge to strip them off. There was nothing moving but the Tinkerbell fluttering of insects in the shafts of yellow sun.

Conscious of the world around us, we spoke rarely and only in soft whispers. We started when the FOB called in with a comms check, worried the drones could barely see us in the bayous. I watched the banks and the water closely. Cheung was fixed on navigational hazards. Tangles and deadfalls. The endless cypress knees. A giant gar nuzzling the skimmer.

And then, sometimes, the forest would thin and there would be air and light. And there we would be, the creek carrying us through conifer-dotted flatwoods and wetlands of palm-leaved palmettos and uprushes of ferns. The occasional cypress domc of flushes of trees, planes and huge *Cladophlebis* ferns and the strange kauri trees. Plane trees hung heavy with drupes, the fleshy fruit surrounded by endocarps tough as PVC.

We saw little in the way of big animals beyond fish. That grated on my nerves. The hammocks, the meadows, both were fine Carcharodontosaur hunting grounds and while we hardly looked appetizing, it nonetheless made us nervous.

The banks of plants crowded in. Loomed over us, casting long shadows. Out of curiosity, I removed my rebreather. The smell was rich, dense. Methane. Silage. Loam. A memory of an animal house during a trip to the zoo.

And then came the crackle and snap of splitting timber.

Something big this way came.

Cheung slid the skiff to a halt. There was a bend in the creek where the sounds were coming from. Crashing. The mooing and guttural, vibrato lowing of animals.

We switched seats, making the skiff rock. Cheung pulled his rifle and checked the chamber. The metal clack of the cycle was strangely human and out of place.

I racked the shotgun. Laid it in my lap and then edged us forward while Cheung lay in the bow. He waved us forward. I slowly twisted the throttle and the carpet of green parted before us.

Slowly, slowly, we took the corner.

'Look at that,' I heard Cheung murmur.

Sauropods. Not giant *Paralititan* but elephant-sized *Aegyptosaurus*, neck to tail, plunging into the creek through holes that blasted in the walls of cypress and rushes. Muddy waters splashed up flanks wrinkled as a rhino's, scaled as a Komodo dragon's. One stumbled. Came up bedecked in garlands of green.

It was like waiting in traffic.

A small boxy head preceded a long arching neck, an osteoderm-speckled back, an endless tail often overlaid with the head and neck of the following Sauropod. The skiff wallowed in the bow waves angling out from the passing of the Aegyptosaurs until, at last, the final thunder lizard sloshed into and out of the creek and we were sat rocking gently as the waves of its passing faded to ripples.

While the jigsaw pieces of floating weed coalesced to cover up the black water once more, I nudged us forward.

It was a bucolic scene that greeted us through the gap rent by the Sauropods in the cypress. In soft and misty morning light, the still dripping Aegyptosaurs were already grazing a meadow of ferns. And they had company. Lurdusaur Iguanodonts. Not the bovine, slender-limbed types we were familiar with but more like horse-headed hippos. Barrel-chested and stout in the arm and leg. Much more at home, like everything here, in the water. They were big, not that much smaller than the Sauropods. *Thalassodromeus* strutted about them, as comfortable on the ground as in the air, little head-dressed men on bat-winged stilts. They stood out white as they snapped at frogs and lizards and worms, gathered expectantly around the heads of the Lurdusaurs as the herbivores ripped out ferns by the roots and left suddenly homeless creatures squirming and easy for the pterosaurs to snap up.

We filmed for a while and Cheung sat, the rifle in his lap, taking pictures instead.

Then, it was time to move on.

While the creek took us to all points of the compass it slowly wended its way progressively north. The forests and meadows thinned out. Hammocks gave way to slough, mudflats, cypress domes and crocodile wallows, acres of twisted branches, stumps, knees, roots, the creek shallow enough that the skiff would ground occasionally and we'd have to gun the engine and aquaplane over water that was little more than surface tension.

By late morning the creek had been swallowed up by a vast flat delta punctured by little islands as far as the eye could see. Some had a single tree and a cluster of scrub bushes beneath it; others sported small forests of cypress, home to creatures to whom the island was their entire world with a climate all its own.

We were deep in the slough now, at the margins of the Bahariya watershed.

I did a comms check. The drones had us in sight and we waved when one buzzed by, high overhead. Out in the open, we felt vulnerable. The Theropods here, like their prey, were as comfortable in water as they were out of it. And we were now in Spinosaur country.

The ghillie suits were by now pretty much redundant. The mist was gone and we were under a climbing sun. The suits might have been cooling but they were heavy and they provided little in the way of camouflage out in the flats.

We stripped them off.

I took in the sea breeze and the smell of salt and rot. The water was brackish now. There were no longer just cypress domes but stands of mangroves as well. And to the north, there was the silver glimmer of the Tethys.

Sitting in the bright Cretaceous sun, the mist left behind in the forests and meadows, it was so still and quiet. Just the susurrations of breeze and water. The occasional whisper of leaves in motion.

It was easy to imagine being the only people on Earth. Which really wasn't that far from the truth.

Cheung chewed a power bar while studying the world with binoculars. He pointed and handed them to me.

'In the water just by the nearest island at one o'clock.'

I focused in. Something sinuously plied the shallows. Small and vaguely serpentine.

'Snake?'

Cheung had picked up his rifle scope. 'Croc, maybe?'

We were both half wrong and half right. It was a snake but was a true croc. It was a terrestrial crocodilian, *Libycosuchus*. It swam like its semi-aquatic brethren but when it hauled up on the island, its legs were long and straight. It trotted across the mud and vanished into a tangle of cypress roots.

The tide was low as we started north again. We followed the deep moats that surrounded the islands and the creeks that spidered around them. The water was murky and beige, rich with sediment, thick with detritus. I caught the occasional glitter of fish, darting into the shadow of the skiff. Darting away again.

And sometimes there was the shadow of something bigger.

While we paused to check our position, there came a clunk and the skiff juddered. Out of some primal instinct, I grabbed the sides and held on for dear life.

Something very large broke the surface just a few feet to our right. A big fish. We never saw what it was and couldn't even guess the type.

It was easy to feel isolated and vulnerable here.

The little creeks solidified into a broader watercourse that led us amongst an archipelago of larger islands thick with mangroves and spike rushes. Pneumatophores, the mangroves' breathing roots, rose like clusters of wooden snorkels from the green water, sometimes hemming us in. It was worse when the waters turned to swamp and thick tangled masses of stilt roots, furred slick with grey periphyton. The maze of roots and branches arched over us and it was so still and magically quiet. Nothing big could hide here, so thick were the mangroves, so we sat and looked about us in wonder. Dragonflies of iridescent red and sapphire hovered and thrummed about us or sat jewel-like on the waxy leaves. Pretty red crabs busied themselves in the mud.

And finally, we left the fairyland to its invertebrate rulers and were presented with tidal flats, the waters now turquoise and emerald where it was just moistening the plains of mud and scum. The islands marching to the sea grew progressively small and all about us were endless stands of mangrove.

Pterosaurs circled to the north-east. Just a few but enough to pique our interest. We weaved amongst the mangroves until we saw a huge fish beached on a little island no bigger than the average living room. It was the biggest fish I'd ever seen. A *Paranogmius*. Twice the length of the skiff. It was mainly head, spine and tail. The rest had been eaten. What little meat was left might have been a juicy pink once but was now black with flies which blew up in clouds when the jabbing beak of the pterosaurs attending the funeral feast speared a scrap here, jerked a slither there, stretching it until the fish snapped away.

The pterosaurs, half a dozen or so *Thalassodromeus* and little *Siroccopteryx*, crept gingerly about the mud, fingers blackened with it, gloriously white wings splattered into modern art. The latter type stood away from the more raptorial *Thalassodromeus* who would screech and threaten if one came too near.

The waters parted.

'Wow,' said Cheung, a masterful understatement.

The *Aegyptosuchus* was twice as long as the island. Its narrow jaws were as long as I would have been lying down beside it. Its long, fluid body was plated in staves of bony armour, layers of it, like a samurai's. Its flanks were more like walls tiled in oval-shaped porcelain. Its tail was long enough to be an animal in and of itself, ridged and plated the way a dragon's might be.

It slid, implacable, up the muddy beach, unconcerned by all about it. The pterosaurs scrambled, a rush of wings to the sky. A horror movie soundtrack of screams and hisses accompanied them until only the flies remained to trouble the dead fish. But even they scattered when the *Aegyptosuchus* snapped its jaws shut around the fish's tail and shook the carcass. A kindling of soft bones snapped and the crocodile gave one gulp, gave two, and a good third of the body was gone. It took the fish's spine. Shook that too, until the head snapped away, by default or design. The *Aegyptosuchus* rolled its canoe-sized head and crunched them shut on the fish head. Its throat pouch hung heavy as it swallowed its catch then it jerked its head back and swallowed the head down.

The croc toothed the spine again but maybe that was unappetizing, for it abandoned it and rolled its head to bite at nothing. With nothing but stinking mud left to tempt it, the mammoth crocodilian sat for a while, but the mangroves were casting shadows and with not even the sun to bathe in, it turned slow as a battleship and slipped into the water whence it came.

There was a heart-stopping moment as the skiff rocked with the passage of the *Aegyptosuchus* but its shadow headed west and there was soon no sign of crocodile, pterosaurs or fish but for the flies supping on the abandoned spine and the few scraps and juices left in the mud.

Excitement over, we sailed on. The water turned greener and greener, more and more salty. Large islands became few, small islands, many. And finally the cypress was gone and all that remained was mangrove flats. To the north, the horizon was the pure emerald green of the ocean, set beneath towering cumulus clouds of pure white.

It was blazing hot, but at last there was a sea breeze. I had to take off my rebreather and take in the cool smell in deep drafts. Pure, unadulterated air. Cheung and I slathered on more sun cream. His olive skin was already darkening to a rich milk chocolate brown. My arms were ochre, and I shook out my hair. I let it ripple in the breeze and for a moment it was like being in a South Pacific dream. I could so easily have lain down in the skiff and let its gentle rocking lull me to sleep.

But now was not the time.

We didn't have far to go now and the route was more as the pterosaur flew rather than the twists and bends of the creeks. I opened the throttle and the bow lifted as the skiff aquaplaned across the flats.

We passed over deep channels amongst the mangroves, skipping across them to take solace in the ankle- or knee-deep shallows, where no marine predator could surprise us and any terrestrial one was visible from a mile off.

The moving map showed where to go and the imagery from the drone showed us what to expect except when a pterosaur took a dislike to it and its controller had to zoom away to avoid damage to either party.

Cheung was watching with binoculars. He saw the pterosaurs first. They hung in the cobalt sky. They could just as easily have been gulls, albatrosses, at this distance, but they weren't.

The slowly swirling mobile of white wings spun about our destination.

Cheung raised a fist and I slowed. The water ahead was an expanse of emerald, a finger of sea probing in from the coast. This wasn't a channel. There were waves and it was wide.

We could tell by the line of mangroves that marked its edge. Real coastal waters.

There was nothing on the map to mark the depth but it was deep enough, we knew, to take the draft of a shark or a Polycotylid, or even a Pliosaur.

Speed was of the essence. Get across as fast as we could. The threat was hitting something. The skiff was tough. Its keel was coloured like a dead tree, of little interest to any predator. But a collision at speed could tip the boat. Send us spilling into the water. We might hit a log. Or we might hit something a little more animated, with jaws as broad as my outstretched arms.

Cheung studied the waters. I absently toyed with the throttle. The silenced engine made no more noise than a sad sigh, but it was louder than the wind and that was the only sound I could hear. The sea breathing.

Finally, he looked back.

'Gun it,' he said.

I pushed the rudder over and spun the skiff about, taking us back the way we'd come then slowly brought us back to face emerald expanse of seawater.

I gunned it.

The skiff picked up speed, bow riding high. Cheung sat back, hands gripping the sides. We were going flat out when we hit sea. The waves were small but they thumped against the speeding hull and the skiff began to buck a little as it planed across the water. My eyes were fixed firmly on the mangroves but Cheung leant from one side to the next. Searching, searching, searching.

But the waters were quiet and we had speed, and then we blasted between the mangroves and I let go the throttle. The skiff slid to a halt but not before there came the rattle of outstretched roots, snapped by our passage.

Cheung smiled. 'Phew.'

I laughed back.

But I checked the map and there were many channels to cross before we made our destination and who knew what we'd find there.

It was time to take it slow.

We crossed the open channels at the narrowest points we could find, ever cautious, Cheung scoping the waters for trouble but finding none.

And slowly we drew ever nearer the place we would hunt those scavengers. We could see the ever-circling pterosaurs then hear them, and once their caws came to us, we stopped on a wide open flat dotted with sprigs of mangrove to consult each other and FOB Deliverance.

We watched the imagery from the drones first. The *Paralititan* carcasses were piled against the seaward side of one of the larger islands; two of the bodies had clogged a channel.

There were no Theropods but the waters around the dead Sauropods seethed. Sharks, dozens of them. Their hazy teardrop-shaped shadows cruised the shallows but there were other shapes, giants far bigger than the sharks. Gars and bichirs, adaptable enough to tolerate brackish, even salt water, had followed the scent of dead flesh from the creeks and bayous, and came out into the open tidal flats of the watershed on the prowl. Tails and fins and great armoured bodies thrashed and churned the water pink with blood and foam, as they tore into the giant carcasses. A beautiful shark, *Cretolamna*, shuddered as its tail lashed back and forth, driving the shark's head deep into a gut cavity, blood boiling out. Horned hybodont sharks jostled the *Cretolamna*, thrashing their heads back and forth as they tore at intestines and stomach, the water green with the Sauropod's semi-digested plant matter.

And it wasn't just fish. Huge crocodilians, not just *Aegyptosuchus* but mighty Sacrosuchids with blue-black metal-looking backs, ignored the sharks and the gars, but fought each other for the best feeding spots.

And not just fish and crocs... Marine reptiles had come in from the warm shallows of the Tethys; Pliosaurs with jaws and teeth bigger than any crocs, flying in with a stately cetacean grace on paddles bigger than the skiff. They were big enough to ignore the biggest crocs, sharks that under more normal circumstances stood a chance of more likely being prey. There were three of them, dominating the scene, staying down to feed, surfacing only to take a breath, otherwise nothing more than massive ambulatory shapes swallowed up by blood and silt and sharks.

There were a few Polycotylids, smaller, more nimble but more nervous, darting in and about the melee, more hopeful of grabbing a scrap or two than fighting it out close in to a carcass.

There were flashes of silver too, as shoals of fish swept in to snap up bloody detritus then darted away.

Strutting about the carcasses where they broke the surface were the folded kite shapes of pterosaurs; *Thalassodromeus* and the great *Alanqa*, with their 25ft wingspans. The former was bolder, more aggressive, feeding right at the zone where water met flesh and they would use their sharp beaks to drive off sharks too curious or too blinded by meat lust that came too close to the pterosaurs.

All in all, it could easily have been some vision of Hell. But it looked like a scavenging Theropod heaven and it's where we needed to be.

But we certainly didn't want to be on that island. We needed somewhere where we could observe the action, not end up being part of it. So, we checked the map and talked to the FOB, who were intensely nervous and wanted to launch the Pink Team.

Call it ego. Call it bad karma. Call it stupidity. Call it what you like, but we declined. No, we were not going to get *that* close. We were not *that* stupid. Yes, we were being careful. Yes, we remembered our training. Yes, we were taking all precautionary measures.

We went back to the map.

There was one island not far from the carcasses, a little to the north-west of the bodies. It was big, big enough for a water-filled hollow at its heart, sans predators, and with a small nesting colony of *Siroccopteryx* around one end. The mangroves formed a dense fringe about its roughly oval shape. We could beach and set up on the south side then wait it out.

The FOB remarked on the soundness of the plan but pointed out that it was now early afternoon and our window of opportunity for sitting, sweating, hot and insect-assaulted while we waited for a Theropod not to show up at all, was closing fast; that we would soon have to leave if we didn't want to be navigating the skiff through the dense Bahariya Everglades at dusk and then night. A moonless one at that.

A valid point, Cheung and I agreed. But we had a hide and food and water enough for a night under the stars.

The FOB offered to once more launch the Pink Team and ferry us back to base.

This back and forthing was interrupted by one of the drone operators. She'd spotted something of interest to the south.

On the drone's camera came *Spinosaurus*.

We watched enthralled. The war colours it carried on its sail told us it was a male. He was huge, and he was why we had come to the Bahariya. Too much *Jurassic Park III* as children. And it was clearly coming our way, following the dead scents northward.

That was all the convincing we needed.

The trip to the island would require time spent in open water so we asked the drone operators to check the route. It was a somewhat futile exercise; what might be clear five minutes before could easily harbour a shark or croc by the time we were passing. I, however, was keen to gauge the odds of running into trouble.

The drone crept overhead and we studied the imagery. The waters were beige or jade green. Not a shadow to be seen.

We decided to chance it. The drone paced us as we took it fast across the flats, faster across open water. Darting across one of the fingers of sea, baitfish were stewing at the surface, their tiny bodies glittering as they leapt from the water with a sizzle.

Something was down there.

I twisted the throttle into the red and skiff flew.

Just as we hit the flats, Cheung pointed over my shoulder. I slowed and looked back.

A dorsal fin sliced the water's surface. Several feet behind undulated the tip of the tail. I could almost see the drone operator shrugging with an 'I told you so'.

But that was the closest to trouble we came and we made landfall on the island. We had trouble finding a suitable place to come ashore, the roots of the mangroves forming dense walls of buttresses and balustrades, palisades of pneumatophores that threatened to skewer the bottom of the boat. But we found a spot where the snorkel roots were small enough and thin enough, and where a stream picked its way through the dense bush, for us to land.

Land, at this point, might have been a little too... hopeful. Land implies solid ground beneath your feet.

This was not solid ground. This was a thick grey mud that covered me above the ankles as I struggled ashore to claim the island in the name of me. I envied the crabs that scuttled out of my way with a gazelle-like ease.

The dense mangroves still had that strange, ethereal quiet once we finally found firmer ground and the mangroves were joined by other hardy, salt-resistant flora. We stood in the shadows for a while and listened. The pterosaur colony was noisy and smelly, and we really didn't want to go out in the open and risk being dive-bombed by angry parents so we unloaded what we could from the skiff, without actually discussing that we would indeed be here for the night. Cheung naturally took the hide and his rifle as priority. I took food and water, torches and sleeping bags. Slung them into a backpack, but left the ghillie suits. I did remember the repellent and the hoods, though. We would be in the lee of the island, with no pleasant sea breeze to keep the biters and bloodsuckers off us.

The mangroves defeated us. There was no way through so we risked the open heart of the island.

We didn't know but we were walking into a yawning hole in the drone coverage. One was watching the progress of the Spinosaur, the other was checking the waters around the *Paralititans*. No one was really paying attention to us; we were safely ashore and we had neglected our own safety by not having one of the operators check out the island first; we had been more concerned with the marine threat. It was a small island after all. I could have crossed it in five minutes. We'd also been lulled by the peace and tranquillity of the mangroves, and their sheer density. What could possibly have been hiding that we or the drones could not have seen, right?

Even had the drones been watching, time was against them. They could watch but that was it. We were, after all, the ones with the guns. An elephant load from Cheung's rifle would shatter the braincase of the largest Theropod. But his Ruger was in its snug case slung over his shoulder. His shotgun was across his chest as was mine.

We fought our way out of the jungle and there was pandemonium. A colony of

Siroccopteryx, giant ugly seabirds with hatchet-like beaks, burst into the air.

I unslung my shotgun.

Not the biggest of the Ornithocheirids by a long shot, they were big enough. I never had any intention of shooting one; they were parents after all and just defending their nests. But a shotgun does make you feel much safer and I would have something at least to jab at them.

It's likely that when the drone was being vectored away to check the channels we were to cross, the cheeky *Rugops* had been paddling in from the west and decided to stop for a breather or a drink. Perhaps it had taken a look at the chaos and carnage being wrought around the carcasses and an instinct for self-preservation dulled the hunger that had brought it here. Perhaps it was there to hunt for pterosaur eggs. Perhaps, perhaps, perhaps. It was unlikely to be trailing us, even though it made landfall minutes after us. Our trail was just the path of least resistance so it was only natural it came in the same way we did.

Whatever.

All I saw was a lot of wings. Heard a lot of noise. The pterosaurs were rolling towards me and I backed away into the security of the mangroves...

The drone was back because I heard someone say, 'Oh shit...' on the comms.

Naturally I assumed he was talking about the infernal chaos of the panicking pterosaurs.

But he wasn't.

There came a crushing pressure on my left shoulder, so

powerful my legs gave out. The shotgun fell from my suddenly nerveless fingers and tangled with the backpack I dropped. You see, I'd figured it was going to be a short walk, so why would I need to put that heavy thing on my back, especially in this heat? I dropped it and straps entwined. I couldn't get my right hand free to absently feel for my left shoulder. All I could do was look.

A scaly snout and flaring nostrils.

And there was the awful realization that there were teeth digging into my shoulder. There was no pain as such. Just that crushing pressure and the grinding of bone that felt like someone drawing fingers across a blackboard.

I don't really remember very clearly what happened. Like the survivors of car wrecks or plane crashes, the mind has a way of blocking it all out and pretending it didn't happen.

I've seen the footage since, of Cheung as he turned and there I am, suddenly being lifted up into the air by the *Rugops*. I have to watch with the sound down; the scream in Cheung's voice always terrifies me.

I see him swing the shotgun up. There's a puff of white as the gun coughs. The Rugops' head glances. It looks as if the baton round hit the thick bone on the roof of his skull.

Didn't make a dent. The Theropod just looks perplexed as I thrash and flail. My mouth is wide open. I'm screaming. The first time I watched it with sound, it was more like a dog whistle. It was amazing I could produce something so high-pitched.

White wings keep flashing through the shot. What's not clear is if the pterosaurs are attacking or panicking. Bit of both, probably.

There's not much to see from the drones. Just a lot of flapping.

On Cheung's camera, he takes his time. Aims. The gun

blasts white smoke again. You can actually see the round ricochet off the armour around the Rugops' eye.

That's about the same time it shakes me and my left arm parts company with my shoulder.

I do remember what happened next.

I remember sky and pterosaurs and the sound of the gunship pilot's voice. He was yelling, 'Guns, guns, guns!' There was almost glee. Maybe this was the first time he'd got to use his cannon.

Made no difference to me.

I just remember the dinosaur's cold, dead eye as it bent down slowly and almost gently took my right leg in its mouth.

Then he shakes me. I get swept back and forth like he's using me to sweep away his tracks.

I remember the snap of my shin bone. Or maybe I imagined it. There was so much noise I could not possibly have heard. The *Rugops* ate my leg.

From Cheung's camera, he gets off two more rounds and the Theropod reacts now. He gives a bellow. That I did hear. For a long time I couldn't go on the subway because I'd hear that roar when the train pulled in.

At this point, I think I passed out.

I never saw the gunship. It fired a burst of five rounds. The *Rugops* was dead before it even knew it. It quite literally ran around like a headless chicken before collapsing and lying there, twitching.

First time I saw the gun camera footage, I actually felt sorry for it. It was just fulfilling its biological imperative. And there I was, with more money than sense, where, according to the laws of nature, I had no right to be.

While the Victor's corpsmen were attending to me, the crew chief cut open the *Rugops* and got my leg back. I never really understood why. Made no difference to me. I wouldn't be using it again and according to everything we'd been told about temporal mechanics, we weren't about to add fuel to the creationist fire when some poor palaeontologist dug up a human tibia in a future fossil.

The next thing I remember was waking up at the FOB. When you have the sort of money I have, time stands still for no catastrophic amputation and I'd already been outfitted with prosthetics. I was as good as new soon after. If not better.

But there isn't a day that goes by where I don't wonder what became of that *Rugops*. His carcass was airlifted back to the FOB. There was a very public dissection and he no doubt provided scope for advanced science, which we should be grateful for, but after that? I assume he was dumped somewhere and left for the scavengers.

Cheung, meanwhile, was given a default kill and has the model head in his study. He never got his other kills and gave up hunting. Too many nightmares afterwards, especially the ones where I'm screaming. I just have an X-ray they took of me at the field hospital. There were tooth fragments in my scapula and coracoid, gone now.

Compared to the *Rugops*, I got off lightly.

Yishan Lo sold off her highly successful movie production company and retired back to her native Singapore. Much of the money she made from the sale she gave to animal charities.

DINOSAUR PARK FORMATION

Period: Late Cretaceous
Age: Mid-Campanian stage (77–74 mya)
Present location: North America
Reserve size: approx 3,400 square miles (a little smaller than Tsavo West National Park)

CONDITIONS

The Dinosaur Park Formation is found on the subcontinent of Laramidia. This narrow strip of land runs along a north–south axis and is rarely wider than 350 miles. It forms what is now the west coast of the North American continent, extending from the Arctic down to Mexico. At this time, a shallow ocean, the Western Interior Seaway, covered much of the interior and split the landmass into Laramidia to the west and an eastern subcontinent, Appalachia.

Temperatures at this time are cooler than earlier Mesozoic stages, but remain higher than modern pre-industrial times, warm enough to prevent glaciation at the poles and allowing ice to form only on the highest mountains. The general cooling was in part due to the lowering of carbon dioxide levels, to about two and a half times higher than present. This may reduce the mandatory need for use of rebreathers, but it remains strongly recommended they are deployed at all times.

GEOGRAPHY AND ENVIRONMENT

Dinosaur Park Reserve is situated roughly where Alberta, Canada is located. To its west is the Magmatic Arc of the early Rocky Mountain chain, at this time still relatively young and studded with a number of active volcanoes. The highest peaks are iced during the period of shorter days, which also precipitates a general cooling and the start of the wet season.

The Rockies also cast a rain shadow over their immediate foothills and the high plains to the east. These plains are several hundred feet above sea level and slope gently eastward. Large rivers running from the mountains form major watercourses which support riverine forests that thin to open woodland and 'fruit prairies' of juniper-like shrubs and ferns. Smaller watercourses desiccate in the dry season leaving soda lakes and restricting greenery to permanent rivers and the forests they support.

These woods and forests are largely angiosperms or flowering plants that have supplanted the evergreen gymnosperms of previous times. Pines, cycads and conifers are still present, but in much smaller numbers; the primary trees are the likes of sycamore, plane trees and maples. In the wet season, the profusion of fruit-bearing shrubs and fields of flowers such as the great carpets of goldfields that flower at the start of the rains, support huge herds of dinosaurs. Many of these ascend from the lowlands to breed on the high plains;

huge nesting colonies of Hadrosaurs in particular can be found, formed from thousands of individuals.

The wet season also sees the soda lakes refill and attract nesting dinosaurs and flocks of pterosaurs and birds as the seasonal rivers return, fed by rain from the west of the Rockies and by meltwater from the higher peaks.

Beyond the rain shadow and the eastern edge of the high plains, the riverine forests thicken as the ground descends into lowlands. There is year-round rainfall and the temperature remains mild, turning the low flatlands into floodplains permeated with great fanning river deltas as the large watercourses break up into small, more numerous ones that feed the subtropical forests.

Much of this low-lying area is punctuated with swampland, lush with lakes, ponds and domes of bald cypress. The streams and creeks here are lined with stands of bur reeds and horsetails and filled with water cabbage, water chestnut, lilies and liverwort.

However, the dominant feature of the floodplains are the rich forests. Large conifers and giant sequoia redwoods form the canopy; as in the uplands, angiosperms dominate the understorey; common trees include katsura, boxwood, maples, willows, ginkgoes, podocarps, plane trees and sycamores. Many are covered in climbing ferns and grape vines. The forest floor is rich with coral ferns, big-leaved *Gunnera* and tree ferns.

Most plants keep their leaves all year, although some in more westerly regions will drop their leaves or needles during the dry season to retain moisture. Even along the easterly coastal regions, the rains fail occasionally.

These forests support the richest diversity of dinosaurs to be found anywhere; herds of them plunder the jungles and woods during the wet season as herds bring the new generation to the lowlands to fatten up and grow fast. They naturally bring with them an arsenal of predators, including two Tyrannosaurs and a whole host of raptors. Other dinosaur types, particularly Ceratopsians, eat their way through the forests as they head north at the end of the wet season. They migrate to nest up in the Arctic regions, making the most of the longer days that encourage a growth spurt in the higher latitudes. When the spurt is over, they migrate back south to see out the dry season in the regions of permanent water along the coastal areas.

The damage these migrating herds do is devastating to the area but by opening up the forests, they provide light for new growth of fast-growing plants. The dinosaurs have also, naturally, left tons of manure to help feed the young plants. Similar devastation also follows the occasional forest fires that sweep the lowlands during particularly long and hot dry seasons. These fires can destroy hundreds of square miles of forest and kill large numbers of animals, especially the young and juvenile who usually stay deep in the trees and thick understorey until big enough to venture out into more open habitats. However, the thick ash left behind by these wildfires fertilizes new plant generations which in turn provide for the next generations of fauna.

Further west the forests give way to tidal flats and marshes, the forests thinning and fans of streams and rivers feeding rich sediment into the Western Interior Seaway. Cypress and mangrove-type plants form a line of islands that protect the coastal flats and prevent the sediment being washed away. There are also long stretches of beach where many animals come to feed along the treelines. Many marine animals come into shore during the wet season, when massive shoals of small fish run into coastal waters to feed on the sediment and the microorganisms it attracts. These fish provide food for larger fish that in turn are preyed upon by a terrifying selection of marine predators, ranging from giant sharks to marine reptiles bigger than the largest terrestrial carnivore. Many marine species also breed in coastal waters. For the truly brave, MHC® does offer marine safaris from a second island-based FOB.

Warning: Volcanic eruption is an occasional threat, but warning should be early enough for safety to be sought.

LICENSED TARGETS

You are licensed to hunt the following species in Dinosaur Park:

GORGOSAURUS

Length: 25ft
Weight: 2 tons
The more common and lightweight of the two Dinosaur Park Tyrannosaurs, *Gorgosaurus* is an adaptable generalist predator. It's rather gracile compared to its heavier-set contemporary, *Daspletosaurus*; its build is more elegant with longer, more graceful legs and a short trunk, complete with one of the Tyrannosaurs' most distinguishable features; the stubby but well-muscled arms and their two clawed fingers. The long tail counterbalances the large head, which although long has a lightly constructed skull (certainly when compared to the massive bones of a *T-rex* skull); the jaws support the usual array of Tyrannosaurid teeth, with the small D-cross-sectioned premaxilla teeth giving way to longer teeth, serrated on both sides, that extend the length of the jaw line. *Gorgosaurus* is also distinguishable from *Daspletosaurus* by the lacrimal horn that grows above its eye.

Gorgosaurs are found across Dinosaur Park, ranging from the foothills of the Magmatic Arc to the high plains and down to the forests and swamps of the coastal floodplains. Their primary prey is the various species of Hadrosaurs that gather in huge numbers throughout the park reserve, but they have few restrictions to their list of prey animals; the one exception appears to be adult Ceratopsians, although even one of these will be taken if it is old or sick. Generally, however, they restrict their hunting of horned dinosaurs to the young and juvenile.

Gorgosaurus is usually solitary but breeding pairs will sometimes stay together following the breeding season. Upland communities use the more open spaces of the high plains to pursue prey; their gracile build makes them faster than most of their prey, especially the heavy-set Hadrosaurs. They will charge herds to make them disperse so they can pick out a sub-adult or juvenile. However, during the dry season, they will risk attacking adults, usually delivering a series of slashing bites to weaken the victim. Under these circumstances, they will also show superficial pack-hunting behaviour. This is a rather informal arrangement; following an attack by a single Gorgosaur on a Hadrosaur, the attacker shadows the victim and will on occasion be joined by one or more – sometimes up to half a dozen – others, who will even deliver their own attacks. Once the prey is sufficiently weakened, a process often accelerated by the presence of more than one Gorgosaur, the pack will jointly attack and dispatch the prey. At this point, fights invariably occur to establish seniority at the kill, the subordinates – even the initial attacker if etiquette dictates – waiting their turn to feed. Interestingly, they will often defend the kill from interlopers, be they other Gorgosaurs or Daspletosaurs looking for an easy meal. This can lead to some brutal fighting. Similarly, the higher-ranking individuals will stay after feeding their fill to see off any potential scavengers, their sheer number perhaps providing as much of a deterrent as more aggressive actions.

Lowland Gorgosaurs are more solitary, the dense forests offering greater success to them as ambush predators. This community of Tyrannosaurs preys primarily on sub-adult Hadrosaurs and young Ceratopsians.

The breeding season for *Gorgosaurus* begins at the end of the dry season (roughly equivalent to that of their Hadrosaur prey); it is usually preceded by disputes between young, territory-less males and those with established ranges. This usually results in the death and injury of many Gorgosaurs but the victors have little time to recover as they have to attract females, usually with vocalizations and, once a female is in range, a visual display of strength.

Pairs stay together for the entire breeding season, raising the brood of 10–20 pups that grow (dependent on food supply) with astonishing rapidity. Nest sites depend on environment; a more sheltered position is preferred but on the high plains, Gorgosaurs will nest in the open, especially if close to a Hadrosaur colony. While raising the young, one parent is always in attendance; at this time, they will take easier, more manageable prey that can be brought back to the nest or easily swallowed and regurgitated for the pups. Most favoured are young or sub-adult Hadrosaurs, but as the nesting season progresses and the adult duckbills become increasingly exhausted from the extended distances they are forced to travel in feeding their own litters, a single adult Gorgosaur will risk tackling an adult if it is wounded, sick or weak.

After leaving the nest, the young are long-legged, lean, downy but big-headed and, proportional to the adults, big-toothed. Though not as quick as ostrich dinosaurs, they are considerably faster than their parents and can outrun most other smaller dinosaurs, especially the young of other species that form the bulk of the pup's diet.

The first five years of a Gorgosaur's life are lived out as an extended childhood in the form of a small juvenile, living in forested areas and preying on insects and small vertebrates, stealing eggs and, as they are quite capable swimmers, even fishing. Few survive this early stage, but those that do suddenly transition to the non-breeding sub-adult that fulfils the ecological role between Tyrannosaur adult and the small carnivores. In this niche, they have proportionally very large teeth, but again this is a particularly tough age when they are more likely to encounter cannibalistic adults and other larger predators, as well as far more aggressive prey. Few survive this period (of roughly four years) without injury. To help them through this time of transition, the sub-adults will sometimes congregate into small packs, usually of a single sex. This is the period when they develop their hunting skills and spend a great deal of time fighting one another.

Following this growth spurt, the sub-adults fledge and become sexually mature and continue to grow but at a much slower rate until they reach full size at about 15 years of age in the females and 20 years in the males.

DASPLETOSAURUS

Length: 30ft
Weight: 3 tons

As widely distributed but not quite as common as *Gorgosaurus*, *Daspletosaurus* is by far the more rugged and robust of the two Tyrannosaur types of Dinosaur Park. Broadly similar to its more lithe counterpart in body plan, its primary differences, aside from colouration, are slightly shorter legs, but longer forearms and a more massive head with a blunt snout – if *Gorgosaurus* looks like a runner, *Daspletosaurus* looks like a brawler using strength rather than speed. It does have pronounced lacrimal horns similar to those of *Gorgosaurus*.

The tougher build is attributable to its primary prey item: horned dinosaurs. These rhino- to elephant-sized herbivores are well armed and have the attitude to go with their array of horns, shearing parrot-type beaks, power and speed. To hunt them requires an equally aggressive temperament and rugged build.

Daspletosaurus is perhaps the most 'tactical' of Tyrannosaurs. It is first and foremost an ambush predator, which does restrict its hunting ranges to areas that provide

The 'ostrich dinosaur', *Struthiomimus*, flees the attentions of a young *Gorgosaurus*.

plenty of cover. It will also hunt regularly in pairs; one often acts as a decoy while the other employs classic 'land shark' tactics, bursting from cover to deliver a serious wound then retiring to safety to let shock and blood loss do their work. These are very simple manoeuvres – hardly the work of a pride of lions – but they are effective, if dangerous for the 'decoy'. Unless the wound is particularly grievous or immobilizing, a wounded Ceratopsian is as likely to be enraged and charge the decoy, who may find itself in a fight for its life. Accordingly, the ambushing Daspletosaur targets the hind legs – a 'mobility' kill – that slows or even immobilizes the prey. The Tyrannosaur may not be as fast as a Gorgosaur but is nimble enough to duck, for instance, the horns of a wounded *Styracosaurus*.

As is often the case with Theropod hunts, one bite is invariably not enough and the long, arduous process of bringing down large prey begins. The pair of Daspletosaurs may also have to face not just the wounded prey but also other Daspletosaurs, alone or in pairs, attracted by the scent of blood, who contest the kill. Life is therefore extremely tough for this species; many sustain injuries not just from their particularly pugnacious prey but also from intra-species fighting.

Lowland communities of *Daspletosaurus* principally feed on Ceratopsians, although they will hunt duckbills and any large animal, even Ankylosaurs, should the opportunity present itself; they will also drive Gorgosaurs from their kills (another source of regular injury). On the high plains, where there is less cover, Ceratopsian hunting is restricted to riverine forests and open woodland with dense understoreys. *Daspletosaurus* will hunt in more open environments but in this case duckbills are the primary prey and, unlike Gorgosaurs, they are quite willing to take on fit and fully grown adults.

Some Daspletosaur communities are known as 'transients'; these are migratory and follow those species that progress along the north–south highways, principally the highland species such as *Einiosaurus*; the transient Tyrannosaurs also nest alongside their prey, in the polar ranges at the start of the growing season. This occurs with the lengthening daylight at the start of the southern dry season. Further south, 'local' populations nest earlier, midway through the wet season when many of the less-migratory lowland Ceratopsians, such as *Styracosaurus* and *Chasmosaurus*, form into large herds and nest in colonies at the edge of the high plains and more open woods.

Sub-adult and sexually immature adults are even more migratory; they fuel their growth by staying in the lowlands at the start of the wet season to hunt around the forest-living species; this fuels a journey to the north in time for the polar breeding season. They then follow the herds back south in time for the dry season, preying on the young, the sick and the exhausted, sometimes forming loose coalitions that enable them not just to practise their hunting skills but also to defend kills from aggressive adults; males will also find themselves targets for fully grown bulls, keen to drive off or cannibalize future competition.

Pairs mate at the end of the dry season but nest later into the wet season. This allows them to hunt around the colony when the adults have often stripped away the good foliage, requiring them to travel further for food for their young. This means many nests are often left unguarded, providing easy pickings, while many adults are exhausted enough to find themselves easy kills for the Daspletosaurs.

When the Ceratopsian superherds form up once the young are old enough to leave the colony, Daspletosaurs similarly leave the nest and the family group follow the herbivores; in the lowlands, the huge numbers of horned dinosaurs, especially the young, make this a happy time for the Tyrannosaurs. For those migrating south, there is similarly a large number of young to pick off, including the sick and large numbers of strays. There are also sub-adults and old adults who make easy prey for ambushes set up by the Daspletosaurs ahead of the herd, usually in riverine forests.

At the start of the dry season, the young are abandoned, usually in the sanctuary of the deep forests. The growth rates of *Daspletosaurus* follow those of *Gorgosaurus*, with an extended juvenile phase for the first five years, followed by a rapid growth spurt to sub-adulthood then reaching sexual maturity at about 15 years old.

Sub-adult Daspletosaurs hunt smaller Ceratopsians such as *Prenoceratops* or *Avaceratops*. These are prickly customers for a young Tyrannosaur, aggressive and very

tough. Some also sport small horns, but all have a powerful beak that can deliver a nasty bite. These smaller versions of the huge Ceratopsians provide the young Daspletosaur with ideal opportunities to fashion their hunting tactics, although many fail the test; a *Prenoceratops* beak can crush a fragile shinbone and the horns of an Avaceratops, no matter that they look paltry compared to the nasal core of a *Styracosaurus*, can stave ribs or crack jaws.

But, alongside the sub-adult, sexually immature Gorgosaurs, these young Tyrannosaurs fulfil the ecological niche that falls between the small raptors and Troodonts, and the adult Tyrannosaur. At this stage in their life, they prey mainly on animals smaller than themselves (including juvenile Tyrannosaurs) before undergoing a major change in their body plan and lifestyle.

The Tyrannosaur, *Daspletosaurus*, is threatened by an angry, quiff-tailed horned dinosaur, *Einosaurus*.

A HORNED DINOSAUR OF YOUR CHOICE

Dinosaur Park plays host to a large number of horned dinosaurs or Ceratopsians, both as resident populations and as migrants passing through. Species are also particular to some environments.

The horned dinosaurs are split into two families, the Centrosaurines and the Chasmosaurines. The former include *Coronosaurus brinkmani*, *Einiosaurus*, *Styracosaurus*, *Achelousaurus* and *Pachyrhinosaurus lakustai*; the latter is represented by *Chasmosaurus irinensis*, *Anchiceratops* and *Vagaceratops*.

Centrosaurines have a number of defining features; they are all, on average, 17ft long (*Einiosaurus* is about 14ft while *Achelousaurus* is about 20ft) and weigh around 2 tons. All have highly distinguishable nasal ornamentation, usually a long horn or, in the case of *Achelousaurus* and *Pachyrhinosaurus*, a boss; *Einiosaurus* is easily recognizable by its nasal horn, which actually curves forward over its beak. The headfrills that are one of the most recognizable characteristics of the Ceratopsians are smaller than those of the Chasmosaurines, but are lined with the epiparietal scutes seen on virtually all horned dinosaurs. However, in many Centrosaurines, these scutes have developed into an array of horns that rise from the top of the shield. Usually it is just a pair, but in the case of *Coronosaurus*, these hornlets are bent forward over the shield and surrounded by a cluster of smaller ornamentations. The most extravagant is, of course, *Styracosaurus*, whose array is a striking fan of horns. Combined with the 2ft-long nasal horn, and the bold markings on its shield and face, this particular species is the most awe-inspiring of the Dinosaur Park Ceratopsians.

Centrosaurines are also the most numerous horned dinosaurs, in some cases travelling in herds of hundreds, even thousands of animals. They are also the most visible, roaming the high plains and open woodlands, or in some cases, passing through the reserve during mass migrations to and from northern regions where some species (*Pachyrhinosaurus*, *Einiosaurus*, *Achelousaurus*) nest.

Chasmosaurines are rarer, with more localized populations; they live in small herds or singularly, in deep forest, marshes and coastal estuaries. These species tend to be smaller than Centrosaurines, around 14ft in length and weighing about a ton and a half. They also tend to have far more flamboyant frills that are much longer and broader, and far more colourful. They are also lined with extensive epiparietal scutes; in this family they do not develop into horns although, in *Vagaceratops*, they do extend forward at top edge of the frill; these features, combined with the frill itself, form a very impressive shield.

Combined with the nasal weaponry and powerful shoulders and elbows, Centrosaurines are pugnacious adversaries for Tyrannosaurs and each other; they have a slightly unusual semi-sprawled gait, the elbows at a slight angle to the body and the forefeet a little further out from the midline than the hind ones. However, this provides a lot of charging, pushing and shoving power. Centrosaurines are stabbers rather than wrestlers and many adults, especially males, carry scars from often-serious injuries on their faces, shields and flanks.

Chasmosaurines lack the large nasal horns or bosses. Instead, they tend to have small brow horns and a small nasal horn, the exception being *Anchiceratops*, which has a long pair of brow horns and a large nasal horn not unlike *Triceratops*.

Generally, though, Chasmosaurines prefer prevention rather than cure; their shields are beautifully coloured and serve to warn off rivals and predators; their environment also tends to make more affirmative action a problem; charging in swamps or marshes, or amongst densely packed trees, is not easy so they prefer to keep trouble at arm's length, which could explain why the Chasmosaurines lost the need for impressive horns. However, their warnings are not all bluff; Chasmosaurines are just as aggressive as their Centrosaurine relatives and if it comes to a fight they will fight, although they tend to use their powerful beaks. In intra-species battles, the smaller horns are still used in battle, the fighting more a wrestling contest than the fencing ones of the Centrosaurines.

No matter the family, all the horned dinosaurs possess a powerful parrot beak that usually ends in a sharp tip; they have no teeth in the front of their jaws but at the back these form dense shearing batteries covered by cheeks. Beak size and jaw length tend to determine ecological niches; a number of Centrosaurines, including *Coronosaurus*, are generalists; other high plains species (*Einiosaurus*, *Achelousaurus*) are low- and mid-range browsers, while the likes of *Styracosaurus* are low-browsers, feeding on woodland and forest understoreys.

Chasmosaurines, with their longer jaws and delicate beaks, tend to be more refined feeders, probing deep into the forest undergrowth and grazing on water plants; they will also chop down reeds and shear off bark. All members of the family could also be classed as semi-aquatic, quite comfortable as they are in water and mud.

Local species of Centrosaurine Ceratopsians all follow the same breeding season, gathering into herds at the end of the dry season; where courtship and mating occurs. This can lead to some spectacular battles between the bulls, who are larger than the females – one of the signs of physical dimorphism between the sexes, the other being the more strident colours on the faces and shields of the males. However, these colours fade after the breeding season and telling the sexes apart can be quite difficult.

Lowland species move out of the dense forests into open woodlands and the edge of the high plains to nest at the start of wet season; reliant less on grazing and more on tougher foliage, they mainly stay close to the dense understoreys but will low-browse fern meadows when it is abundant.

Other species, such as *Pachyrhinosaurus* and *Einiosaurus*, use the abundance of the wet season to fatten up; as the season draws to a close, small herds gather in huge numbers to form 'superherds'; these herds travel up 'highways' along the high plains and coastal routes along the edge of the Western Inland Seaway. As the days lengthen in the sub-polar regions, and the short growing season begins, the migrants nest.

All large Centrosaurines nest colonially. They tend to build simple nests scraped in the ground and lay about 20 eggs. Both parents tend to the young, bringing back wood pulp and vegetation for the sluggish young who put all their energy into growing quickly. Once big enough to travel, the young's rate of growth slows down and the herds reform. The sub-adults and immature individuals stay together for mutual defence while they browse on the wet season growth. However, they join the adults and new calves to once more form superherds. These are not structured like mammalian herds but are loose aggregations, the young staying together in crèches protected by all the adults.

Chasmosaurines nest in smaller colonies, using cypress domes, meadows or sand spits. Again this is for mutual protection but unlike Centrosaurines, once the young are old enough, they head into the dense forest understoreys and marshlands. In a curious twist, the juveniles of *Chasmosaurus* and *Vagaceratops* also sprout large brow horns which then greatly reduce as they approach adulthood. These could make the young look more intimidating to smaller predators and provide more active defences that are replaced by overall size once they enter their near-adult phase.

The young of both families adopt a more omnivorous diet, like small Ceratopsians, and will also scavenge.

OTHER FAUNA

SMALL CARNIVORES

There are a number of small carnivores that inhabit the Dinosaur Park Reserve, each with a more or less unique ecological niche.

The smallest is *Hesperonychus*. With most of its 3ft length taken up with tail, this tiny Microraptorine is arboreal, spending much of its time in the trees and shrubs. A social animal, it travels in small troops; the down of its tail is brightly marked in strips and used as a signalling device between the troop members. In many ways it fulfils the role of a small monkey, and eats a similar diet: insects, small vertebrates, the eggs and chicks of birds and small dinosaurs, and even fruit.

Bambiraptor is a common raptor frequently seen in the woods and high plains, where it functions as a generalist predator. About 4ft long and 30lbs in weight, it is well armed, with a battery of sharp teeth in strong jaws, each hand with three fingers equipped with long claws, and a well-developed sickle claw on each of its hind feet. This battery of weapons enables it to take on a broad spectrum of prey animals, from insects to small Ceratopsians and Protoceratopsids, and juvenile Hadrosaurs. It is also an opportunistic scavenger, bold enough to steal from much larger predators, and, during the wet season, will even take Tyrannosaur eggs if the opportunity presents itself.

Much rarer is *Dromaeosaurus*. About 7ft long and 30lbs, it is a solitary lowland predatory. Its head is robust, with a blunt snout and stout teeth, and as such serves as the raptor's primary weapon. Although athletically built, its forested habitat no longer requires it to chase down prey and it has become an efficient ambush predator whose sickle claw – the signature weapon of the raptor clade – has become far less prominent. It hunts small- to medium-sized predators, including Protoceratopsids, small Ornithopods, Struthiomimids and even other, smaller carnivores.

Far more common, and a regular sight for any hunter is *Saurornitholestes*, a lowland diurnal predator 4ft long; it preys mainly on small animals, including mammals, birds, juveniles and hatchlings, but is also a regular scavenger.

Troodonts have a similar diet but are largely nocturnal. With their big eyes and binocular vision, they are very adept at hunting mammals, but in the wet season, they bolster their diet with hatchling Hadrosaurs and Ceratopsians. They hatch their own chicks close to nesting colonies and use the cover of darkness to sneak in and steal eggs and babies. There are two species, *Troodon* and *Saurornithoides*, both around 8ft long; however, the former favours lowland, forested habitats while the latter is mainly found in the high plains.

CAENAGNATHIDS

These bizarre yet beautiful small dinosaurs are amongst the most colourful of the Park's inhabitants. A little over 4ft at the hip, they are long-legged, their hind claws straight, and about 5–7ft long. Their arms appear more wing-like, supporting long feathers, and fold snuggling against the body, while their tails are short, more like a pygostyle, and support a cluster of long feathers. However, their most striking feature, physiologically, is their head. They sport curved toothless beaks above which is a cassowary-like crest. Males are not only larger but also sport larger crests; they are much more brightly coloured, the females, not required to engage in gaudy courtship displays, being far duller but also suitably camouflaged in their forest habitat. The males will also engage in fairly heated combat during the breeding season, and are quite capable of inflicting serious wounds on one another with powerful kicks from their taloned feet. However, when faced with predators, Caenagnathids favour speed where possible as a means of defence.

Primarily herbivores, these dinosaurs use their strange jaws to pluck fruit and nuts, but in the dry season, when these food sources are not as freely available, they will also happily become omnivores, taking insects, shellfish, small vertebrates and even eggs and hatchlings of birds and dinosaurs. There are two species of Caenagnathids in the Park: *Chirostenotes*, the larger of the two at about 7ft long, and *Caenagnathus*, which is only about 5ft long. The former is more widely distributed, found up in the riverine forests of the high plains as well as the lowlands. The latter is restricted mainly to the deep forests and marshes of the deltas.

HADROSAURS

Hadrosaurs, the famous duckbills, are the most numerous animals in Dinosaur Park. There are a number of species, divided between the high plains and Magmatic Arc foothills, and the lowlands. The former types are migratory, while the lowland types have more localized populations. They are also fewer in number, the upland species forming herds that can be staggering in numbers, tens of thousands, sometimes even more.

Hadrosaurs have a fairly generalized form; their long forearms appear 'mittened', with all the fingers except the thumb covered in a glove of skin, and they are not much shorter than the hind limbs. As such, they are habitually quadrupedal, although prefer to run on their hind legs. Their tails are long and quite deep; their necks are short and curved, and thickset like a horse or bison. This is a convergent feature of herbivores that are low-browsers or grazers.

Hadrosaurs also share the same style of dentition, with hundreds of teeth compressed into powerful grinding batteries at the back of the jaws; these can grind up the toughest plant matter. Duckbills have no front teeth; instead they have the duck-shaped beak that gives them their common name; the edge of the beak is rough keratin and used to pluck and pull up vegetation.

The head is the one area where Hadrosaurs differ. They can be split into two types: crested and un-crested. The former include the upland *Hypacrosaurus intermedius* and lowland *Lambeosaurus*; the un-crested by *Maiasaura* in the uplands and *Prosaurolophus* and *Gryposaurus incurvimanus* from the lowland forests.

Hypacrosaurus' crest is semi-circular in shape, while Lambeosaurus' is similar but shaped more like a hatchet blade, with a spike-like process protruding from its rear. This serves as an attachment for a ribbon-like crest that runs down its back and tail, a feature also seen in *Hypacrosaurus*. The crests in both animals are hollow and filled with curved tubes that feed into the nostrils. These tubes serve not just to increase the surface area of the nasal cavity, giving these duckbills a very acute sense of smell, but also act as resonating tubes. As a result, the calls of these animals are very loud; the noise generated by several thousand Hypacrosaurs is quite deafening and can have a disorientating effect on predators, serving as a passive defence. However, this species is lacking in sexual dimorphism beyond a slight variation in size, the female being larger; this generic body type is a feature seen in many animals that travel in large numbers, including dinosaurs. However, *Lambeosaurus* is somewhat different, the males being larger and with far more pronounced crests (the males are also much more brightly coloured, unlike in *Hypacrosaurus* where the colours in both sexes are more or less uniform). In the dense forest, strident calls help attract mates and once the female is in sight, the bright colours seal the deal. And while both can be alluring to females, they also serve as deterrents to rival males.

These same strategies are seen in the non-crested Hadrosaurs. The monomorphic *Maiasaura* live in massive herds on the high plains; these are the largest aggregations of dinosaurs in the Park, gathering in herds tens of thousands strong. Following the breeding season, the young and adults alike fatten up on the fern prairies and upland meadows before migrating to the northern regions in time for the growing season. They then head south, the herds dissipating during the dry season before once more convening just prior to the arrival of the rains in time for courting to begin once more.

Prosaurolophus and *Gryposaurus* inhabit the low forests, marshes, swamps and coastal regions; they live in small herds that are mainly localized to the lowlands, although some populations will travel to the high plains during the wet season to graze the lush new growth. Both species are dimorphic in size and colour, while the males sport large and brightly coloured bladders on their arched nasal crest akin to those seen in elephant seals. These are used to generate loud roars in the same way *Lambeosaurus* uses its crest, and for similar reasons.

The result of all these devices is that the mating season in Dinosaur Park is an amazingly colourful and noisy affair!

As with the Ceratopsians, the large number of species present is only possible because of a division of ecological niches. In the high plains and foothills, *Maiasaura* is essentially a grazer, using its broad beak to crop ferns and ground-covering plants; *Hypacrosaurus* is a low-browser, feeding on cycads, tree ferns and the understorey vegetation of the upland riverine forests.

In the lowlands, *Gryposaurus* fulfils the role of low-grazer, while *Prosaurolophus*, one of the largest of the Hadrosaurs with males reaching as much 30ft in length, is an opportunist that is quite capable of felling small trees as well as browsing low shrubs and ground-covering plants. *Lambeosaurus*, meanwhile, is a capable mid-range browser but, when rising onto its hind legs, it can also browse as high as any dinosaur in the Park.

While showing diversity in feeding stratagems, when it comes to breeding, Hadrosaurs follow more or less the same pattern, the real difference coming down to the matter of numbers. All species nest colonially, but upland types have nesting areas that are vast, as would be expected from the more open terrain. Lowland species move from dense forest to woodland and meadows, or even coastal beaches, to nest; however, their colonies are somewhat smaller – in the tens. The upland colonies, however, number in the hundreds, the thousands or even the tens of thousands. They can cover dozens of square miles, filled with nests approximately one Hadrosaur body length apart – a strategy adopted by all species. The nests are bowl-shaped and lined with vegetation. Around 20 eggs are laid at the start of the wet season and the young are attended by both parents. The hatchlings themselves stay in the nest for some time; they are initially sluggish, directing all their energy into growing as quickly as possible. To this end, they are fed by the parents, one of them daily joining herds which head out from the colony to graze and/or browse the surrounding vegetation; the other parent stays behind to protect the young from predators and the weather. These duties are usually rotated on a daily basis.

The need to feed the hatchlings' high-tempo growth s mean that the adults strip the vegetation surrounding the colony very quickly; they then find themselves locked in a race between keeping up with the young's growing demands for food with the need to travel further and further away from the nest, where they risk attack from the ring of predators that tends to surround the colony; they also have to contend with growing exhaustion, which in turn makes them weaker and more vulnerable to predation. Accordingly, as the nesting season progresses, losses amongst the adults rise, the result of which is that infant mortality rises as single parents struggle to provide enough food for the young while also being forced to leave them unguarded. Many hatchlings fall to the huge number of opportunist predators who gather in very large numbers around the colonies. Those nests at the edge of the site are especially vulnerable; as such, there is often very serious fighting and theft amongst the adult Hadrosaurs at the start of the laying season; a duckbill will destroy the unguarded eggs of a better-positioned neighbour, who will then abandon the nest, leaving it free for the taking. Those left on the outside must, by day, contend with raptors, pterosaurs, Protoceratopsids and varanid lizards, some of which would dwarf the modern Komodo dragon. By night Troodonts and mammals stalk in to steal eggs, hatchlings and young. Disease is also a potential menace, especially those of the giant upland sites. And, of course, there is the ever present threat of Tyrannosaurs, who have their own nestlings to feed.

However, late in the season, starvation becomes the true grim reaper; as many parents succumb to the various forces arrayed against them, the fast-growing young go hungry and starve quickly; a single parent will abandon its brood if it instinctively knows it cannot provide for the young, preferring to risk waiting to try next season than fight a losing cause. Others, too sick or too exhausted, stay and die with their young.

A nest colony late in the season can be an amazing and melancholic sight – but is the perfect place to stalk Tyrannosaurs...

ANKYLOSAURS

Both families of Ankylosaurs are represented in Dinosaur Park: the Ankylosaurid *Euoplocephalus* and the Nodosaurid *Edmontonia* (although the species is unclear) and *Panoplosaurus*. These are amongst the most spectacular of the Park's residents.

Euoplocephalus is a wonderfully strange looking beast. At around 18ft long, it weighs over 2 tons, much of that weight taken up with its incredible array of armour. Its broad head features triangular spikes at the back corners of the skull and on the cheeks; larger spikes run down the neck and are largest across the shoulders. Lines of scutes run down its wide-bodied abdomen which is covered in layered plates of armour made from pebble-like scales. The scutes enlarge into spikes once more at the base of the tail.

The base of the tail itself is fairly inflexible but the rest is quite elastic; this is to help it wield the huge club it sports at the tip. This impressive weapon is made up of over several bosses of bone, one particularly large one on either side of the tip and several smaller ones in between. While the armour is largely defensive, the club is very much offensive, the musculature of the tail enabling the Ankylosaurid to whip or lash the club with a flick of the base. Tyrannosaur shins beware...

Impressive as the armour is, *Euoplocephalus* also uses bold colours that serve as a warning to its potential predators (mainly the Park's Tyrannosaurs, particularly *Daspletosaurus*). Clearly, prevention is better than cure, *Euoplocephalus* adopting the strategy of many apparently dangerous animals, be they bombardier beetles or sea snakes, that they are not to be trifled with. It is also a relatively mild-mannered dinosaur unless riled but then it can afford to be. It is not built for lightning battles; its short legs are quite capable of a slow gallop, but this is rarely put to use. Its body meanwhile has a broad girth to accommodate its sizeable gut, which acts as a fermentation vat for breaking down plant matter. Its teeth are small and, in combination with its broad toothless beak, are used simply to pull vegetation into the mouth. Diet is restricted to soft plants, which in turn limits the dinosaur's habitat; it is generally found in forests, marshes and swamps, where it grazes on water plants and ground-covering growth. As such, *Euoplocephalus* is comfortable in water, its broad gut making for an excellent flotation device. It will even swim out to cypress domes and mangrove islands to graze in coastal regions.

The nostrils of *Euoplocephalus* are unusual, the nostrils themselves broad while the nasal passage is convoluted inside the animal's large skull. Its eyes are small, relatively speaking, and its sight poor, so these nasal passages give the Ankylosaurid an enhanced sense of smell. However, they also double as resonators that help produce deep low-frequency calls that *Euoplocephalus* uses to communicate. These sounds travel far in the enclosed forest environments it frequents and even through water. A mainly solitary animal, the only times these calls are put to good use is during the mating season when males establish territories and invite females into them. They will also attract rival males and if push quite literally comes to shove, intra-species battles involve shouldering and hitting the opponent with the tail club, especially around the head. This may explain why the upper eyelids of *Euoplocephalus* are armoured!

After a perfunctory courtship and delicate mating, pairs go their separate ways. Females nest alone in dense undergrowth and the young, hatched bearing light armour, are abandoned soon after birth. The young are omnivorous and will often stay together in small herds of young from the same clutch. After an initial growth spurt that sees their armour develop quickly, they then go their separate ways.

Nodosaurids are just as impressive and equally well-adorned with armour, spikes and colours as their Ankylosaurid cousins, but lack a tail club. They more than make up for this in the huge cuirass of pebbled armour that covers its wide back, edged in large scutes, and the array of massive forward-pointing shoulder spikes they sport. That said, they are in general more lightly armoured and have longer limbs, and both types have more narrow snouts; the jaws end in a keratin beak but the teeth are small like those of Ankylosaurids. However, Nodosaurids are more fussy low-browsers, not the broad-shovelling soft-plant grazer that *Euoplocephalus* is. Nodosaurs tend to favour shrubs, ferns, fruit and seeds; to accommodate their diet, they are more active, *Edmontonia* being the most widely distributed and most common of all the Park's Ankylosaurs. It tends to spend most of the dry season in the lowlands, browsing in around more permanent watercourses, swamps and marshes, but in the wet season, they migrate out in the open woodlands and high plains, to graze the fern prairies and riverine forests. *Edmontonia* is also the most social of the Ankylosaurs, sometimes travelling in loose aggregations of a few animals in more open environments; this is presumably for mutual protection.

Panoplosaurus is the rarer of the two Nodosaurids, restricted largely to the lowland open woods and the deep forests (not so much the swamps and marshes) where it is a solitary low-browser.

The rains bring the Nodosaur mating season, which follows a similar pattern to that of *Euoplocephalus*. However, intra-species fights are a little different, requiring that the males lock their shoulder spines and engage in shoving matches. A different strategy is employed when warding off predators. Nodosaurs crouch low and turn to keep the shoulder spikes pointed at the aggressor. The only way a Tyrannosaur can really kill an Ankylosaur is to flip it on its back but their broad abdomens, low centres of gravity and sheer weight, combined with tail clubs and spikes, make this a difficult task and it tends to be only a desperately hungry or curious juvenile who would risk attacking these impressive animals.

LEPTOCERATOPSIDS

There are several small-horned dinosaurs in the reserve and these should be avoided where possible. Fulfilling the ecological niche of pigs such as forest hogs, peccaries or warthogs (depending on the environment), they are aggressive and resilient, certainly not to be trifled with. It's also wise never to leave food around if you are in a known Leptoceratopsid habitat as this is just asking for trouble. They are considered herbivorous, using their parrot beaks, deep, well-muscled jaws and shearing-blade teeth to crop even the toughest plants; they will also use the beaks to slice off tree bark and wrestle down saplings.

However, plant matter is not all they will eat; they are habitual omnivores. They will eat the eggs and hatchlings of other dinosaurs, and will scavenge, their shearing teeth batteries quite capable of breaking down bone.

One of the most common of these Ceratopsids is *Prenoceratops*. About 4ft long and about 40lbs in weight, it lives in small troops in the forested lowlands and open woodland. In the wet season it largely restricts their diet to fruit, nuts and shoots except during the nesting season of larger dinosaurs, when it will regularly raid colonies to steal eggs and newborns, but also scavenge dead and dying young. In the dry season, it supplements its diet with carrion on a more regular basis and will even drive smaller predators from their kills.

Unlike their larger relatives, *Prenoceratops* nest in single pairs, usually in the deeper forests. Both parents attend the nest until the young are old enough to leave it when they are abandoned. The juveniles stay together, usually forming new troops.

There are other larger types that inhabit the open woods and high plains; these are solitary animals that are much rarer and seem taxonomically close to *Montanoceratops*. Around 8ft in length, they avoid the open plains and meadows during the dry season, spending most of their time in open woodlands and riverine forests; however, when the rains arrive and the new growth provides better cover, they will move out into more exposed environs. They are predominantly low-browsers, but are also aggressive scavengers and have been known to actively prey on small and juvenile dinosaurs, including young Tyrannosaurs.

STEGOCERAS

Approximately 7ft long and weighing around 80lbs, this rather striking dinosaur belongs to the domed-headed Pachycephalosaurs. Relatively common, it inhabits the lowland forests and woods, and the upland riverine forests, rarely venturing into open habitats. Easy to recognize because of its domed head and back mane of high, densely packed quills, *Stegoceras* travels in small single-gender herds that only come together into larger aggregations during the mating season.

The sexes are dimorphic, the manes and domes of the males brightly coloured; they are also generally larger than the females, whose domes are not as well-developed as the males, giving them a more flat-headed appearance. Despite its quite fearsome appearance, the dome is rarely used to ward off large predators; speed is the most common defensive strategy and while not exactly fast, they can generally outrun the larger Tyrannosaurs. Smaller predators, however, can be handled with a sudden charge and butt to the flank.

The mating season is when the dome comes into play the most, used to settle disputes over females. Usually, one bachelor herd will join up with a single group of females, but usually only the biggest and boldest in the group get to mate. Battles can also erupt if a second bachelor herd tries to steal the females. In this case, serious brawls can erupt between a dozen or more males.

Once the mating is done, the exhausted males return to their nomadic existence. The females nest colonially; when the eggs hatch, a number will stay behind to guard the young while the other females leave to browse. Any food brought back is distributed amongst all the young. This seems to be a strategy to encourage only the strongest to feed; the larger or more belligerent hatchlings will bully the smaller ones away.

The babies are born flatheaded, the dome developing only as they approach sexual maturity. They are also precocial and leave the nest soon after hatching, the infants forming a single crèche escorted by all the females. The smaller, less well-developed young are left behind or fall behind, so that the females are able to invest what parental care they can in the stronger, more healthy juveniles.

However, once they reach sub-adult status, the young are abandoned; they usually separate into single-sex herds that stay in dense forest until they attain adulthood and begin to frequent more open habitats.

STRUTHIOMIMUS

These elegant and athletic dinosaurs are the fastest in the reserve. They are built for speed, with their lower legs much longer than their thighs, which are well muscled, to provide power when running.

The number of species in the Park is unclear; there appear to be two types, one very common on the high plains and mountain foothills, the other frequently found in the lowland open woods and meadows. These could be separate genus, perhaps *Ornithomimus* and *Struthiomimus*, or perhaps two members of the same genus, in this case, *Struthiomimus*. The problem is that they are both very similar physiologically except in colouration. Both species are around the same size, around 12ft in length and weighing over 300lbs, but, in the upland type, females are distinguishable by their almost golden down which darkens in the wet season; the lowland females have a barred plumage of white and dark grey. Both types are also dimorphic; the males of the upland type have white bodies but with long golden and orange down on their neck and the long vanes of their forearms. The lowland males are black with red faces and legs. Where their territories overlap, they seem quite comfortable in each other's presence.

Whatever the result of this taxonomic conundrum, these are strikingly beautiful dinosaurs.

Struthiomimids are habitual omnivores, eating whatever the season has to offer, and can be handled by their toothless beaks. At the start of the wet season, they feed on the glut of nuts and fruits, new shoots and flowers, and the insects and small vertebrates they attract. In the dry season, they will use the three long, clawed fingers of their long forearms to scrabble for seeds and tubers, insect grubs, burrowing mammals and lizards; they will also tear at dead logs, breaking open the bark and wood to feed on the many small creatures to be found in them.

Conversely, Struthiomimids are popular prey for many small- to medium-sized predators, especially the gracile young Tyrannosaurs, and in particular Albertosaurs. However, they have to be caught first, and the appropriately named 'ostrich mimics' have been clocked at over 35mph on open ground. Naturally they stay away from more confined habitats, except during the breeding season. They also travel in small flocks. When feeding, one member is always on sentry duty; Struthiomimids have large eyes and excellent vision, and it is hard to take them by surprise. As a result, the most that many predators see of these fleet dinosaurs is a disappearing cloud of dust.

Courtship for both Struthiomimids begins at the end of the dry season. There is usually one male per flock and he must fight off all other suitors who may try to supplant his authority. Usually, the matter can be settled with a strutting display to the interloper, but should that fail, males will fight, using pecks and powerful kicks from their hind feet, which are tipped with long but blunt claws; these can inflict serious injuries (and can be used against small predators).

The successful male mates with all the females in the flock, who nest close together, if not actually colonially. They feed up at the start of the wet season and fast while awaiting the hatching of the young. Around 10–15 eggs are laid in a mounded nest of vegetation constructed by each female. The young are precocial at birth and leave it very soon after hatching; the females time their laying so that all the members of the flock hatch together. They then convene into a single crèche protected by all the females and the male, who may even have other sexually immature males in attendance. These young bachelors are chosen by the male and one of them will supplant him should he die or become too old (the latter quite unlikely...).

The young grow very rapidly and stay with the flock; mortality is high and the survivors leave or are driven off at the start of the next mating season. These sub-adults usually form their own flocks.

HYPSILOPHODONTS

These small Ornithopods are a common sight in Dinosaur Park; it is easy to shoehorn them into the ecological niche of small mammalian herbivores such as gazelle or deer. They are, like their mammalian counterparts, usually very fast and often travel in small flocks (or herds); however, their powerful hind legs are not just for running; combined with long, stout forearms, they are effective burrowers. Upland species such as *Orodromeus* burrow around high-altitude lakes and soda flats. They usually live in pairs or small family flocks; the burrow is abandoned at the start of the wet season and nesting occurs above ground, colonially. The precocial young are then gathered in a single crèche and the herd descends onto the high plains and woods, moving and feeding together for mutual protection until the start of the dry season. Then the herd disbands into the small family units who return to their upland burrows to see out the worst of the dry season, scratching out a living on seeds, nuts, tubers and even insects.

In the lowlands, the powerful hypsilophodont foot has been put to a use other than propelling the animal at high speed. In *Parksosaurus*, the toes splay out to support the animal on the soft ground of the marshes and swamps that it inhabits. Like its upland relatives, it too is a burrower, digging into the banks created by tangles of cypress tree roots and even commandeering old crocodilian burrows. The males are particularly brightly coloured.

CROCODILIANS

As with any Mesozoic environment, crocodilians are an ever present threat should a hunter venture close to the water.

The most common types are the alligatoid *Albertochampsa* and *Leidyosuchus*. These appear very similar to modern alligators, especially the former; the latter is more crocodile-like. They are both generalist hunters, although *Albertochampsa* tends to favour ambushing small to medium dinosaurs. Both grow to about 20ft or more, on average, but much larger specimens have been seen. Both should also be considered dangerous.

The other 'crocodilians' are the Champsosaurs; there are numerous species in the Park, although they rarely exceed 10ft in length and most don't grow beyond 5ft. These reptiles are not actually related to crocodilians but belong to an order known as the Choristodera. Physically, they closely resemble gharials, and they seem to be fulfilling the same ecological niche in the Campanian of Laramidia as that of crocodilian piscivores. They are generally harmless unless provoked.

There is also one other type of true crocodilian that should be considered, especially if in estuarine areas. *Deinosuchus* is rare in the reserve, generally inhabiting the more southern deltas, but it does occasionally appear further north, favouring the deltas and bayous of river estuaries. *Deinosuchus* is a monster, growing to as long as 40ft; its incredibly powerful jaws sport huge conical teeth that are quite capable of crushing the skull of the largest Tyrannosaur and its prey includes the biggest duckbills and horned dinosaurs. It is also a 'salty'; it can be found in the coastal waters of the Western Interior Seaway where it will eat large marine turtles and other reptiles; it also uses these coastal waters as a highway along the Laramidia coastline.

Although an effective swimmer, *Deinosuchus* has large bony scutes on its back that not only provide armoured protection but also serve as anchor points for muscles and connective tissue that bear the load of the croc's massive frame. This enables it to move on land; it is not particularly fast and it is not really capable of terrestrial hunting – it's too big and cumbersome for that. However, it will happily come ashore to scavenge, should the opportunity arise.

It goes without saying that a human close to the water's edge in areas known to be frequented by *Deinosuchus* is at risk; you may appear little more than a snack but it pays to stay clear of coastal waters where possible.

CONCLUSION

There can be little doubt that Dinosaur Park offers the richest, most colourful selection of dinosaurs in any of the MHC® Reserves, and hosts some of its most awe-inspiring sights in spectacular scenery. But it is also perhaps the most dangerous of MHC®'s hunting reserves; there are not just two exception predators, in the Tyrannosaurid shapes of *Albertosaurus* and *Daspletosaurus*, but a number of smaller carnivores and very aggressive omnivores and herbivores. Be warned!

THE HIDE

(Written by Nicci Holmes for the ebook collection, Green Inferno, *edited by Jack Shannon. Used with permission.)*

Our greatest failing that day was that we were nothing but tourists. We were simply in love with the place and with the idea of hunting there. Enamoured as such, we forgot so many fundamentals, made so many mistakes. All the training, all the lectures and simulations, it all came to nothing and Cassandra died. The biggest predator I'd ever faced was a lion. With the best will in the world, TIT can't prepare you for something as devastating as a *Daspletosaurus* up close. Seeing it in the flesh, smelling that dead meat smell, looking into the casually indifferent amber-coloured eye ... it freezes your finger on the trigger...

Of course, the lesson I'd love to pass on is listen to those who know better. We had woken early, too excited to sleep. I'd unzipped the tent and we'd stepped out into the morning. There was a dawn chorus, bird songs I'd never heard, birds whose wings may have sported claws and whose beaks may have been lined with teeth.

Not that it mattered. We couldn't see for shit. The fog was thick and the rain was heavy. Nested safely amongst the sentinel trunks of giant sequoias, we were just dripped on steadily, but out beyond the umbrella of the canopy, we could see the mist swirling of its own volition, as there was no breeze to speak of, and the rain was falling straight down.

We didn't care. We were about to enjoy our first day in Dinosaur Park. We nibbled a quick breakfast, checked the guns, and slung on the ghillie suits. Then we checked in with the FOB Good Mother. Their protests were even more persistent than the rain. Vis was for shit, they said. The coverage from the drones was one eye blind. The Pink Team didn't like it. The hard deck was as low as the canopies of the tallest trees was high. Intakes suddenly clogged with leaves and branches, they could auger in before they knew it. Then where would we be?

I pointed out that they would still get paid whether we died or not. Good Mother's commander replied that the reason why the FOB crews were paid up front for the full four weeks was because so many rich assholes arrived in the Mesozoic and chose to forget everything they were taught. Killers they may have been in the boardrooms; generals they may have been on the movie set or in the fashion house, supping champagne whilst ordering their minions about like they were parachuting into Normandy, but generally Theropods were unimpressed by stock portfolios or star billing. High-handed and arrogant, CEOs died quick and violent deaths. So, the crews started asking for the money up front.

It was all very valid and salient, but come on, we were in the Campanian. We were like Neil Armstrong taking his one giant leap for mankind. He didn't have top cover. He'd just done the Right Thing. He had the Right Stuff. And so did we.

And so, the Pink Team stayed grounded. The choppers were hot-cocked and ready to rock on alert five. The aircrews were no doubt watching our camera feeds with disinterest or disdain, but Cassie and I convinced ourselves they were ready to spring into action at a moment's notice – that moment when we'd naively wander into trouble, by which time it would almost certainly be too late anyway. As it turned out, it was.

I had my pads and my pencils in my Bergen. I could have drawn constantly. Sometimes the clouds would thin enough for weak sunlight to turn glades into fairyland dells. The redwood forest towered over us, cypress and maples and katsura gathered around them like children around a mother's apron. This was one of the last stands of forest at the eastern edge of the high plains; head west and you met the flats and foothills of the Magmatic Arc; to the east, the long, slow drop to the lowland river deltas and then the blue of the Cretaceous Inland Seaway. Cycads, *Dicksonia*, the great spreading fronds of *Gunnera*, a verdant skirt of ferns and flowers, billowed over the ground and we waded through it. Sunflowers burst amongst the green. Creeping ferns and vines laden with grapes strangled deadfalls and upturned roots.

It made me think of Conrad. 'Trees, trees, millions of trees, massive, immense, running up high; and at their foot, hugging the bank against the stream, crept the little begrimed steamboat, like a sluggish beetle crawling on the floor of a lofty portico. It made you feel very small, very lost, and yet it was not altogether depressing, that feeling.'

I felt like that steamboat.

We picked up a stream that gurgled playfully as it skipped over its bed of smooth pebbles. The rocks were green with algae but the water was cool and clear, perhaps meltwater from the Magmatic Arc. I was tempted to bend down and take a mouthful. But then I remembered the alien-killing creatures that swarmed and multiplied in a single drop and thought better of it.

We didn't move like hunters. More like ramblers. All we needed was a Labrador. We trudged along the stream's edge, spongy with club mosses, liverwort and water chestnut, bur reeds and moss, filigree-covered horsetails. Ponds grew from the side of the stream and were roofed with water cabbage and lily pads and *Pistia*. Willows and fruit-laden plane trees gathered around them, boxwood spilling about them.

Here was a place where it was easy to fall in love with green. I forgot to be a hunter and became a naturalist. It was strange to imagine a place where there was no sign of people. You could walk in the woods of home, the deepest woods, and you'd still find a rusting can or an abandoned shopping cart. An old fire surrounded by beer bottles and cigarette butts. Here there was nothing but the footprints Cassie and I left in the soft ooze as we studied the surrounding forest, not with field craft eyes but with those of a child at Christmas, bug-eyed with wonder.

The stream made a slow descent north-eastward. As it progressed, it split, split again, split once more. The great redwoods gave way to woodland and thick, dense shrubs. Out of the overcast leant by the sequoia, the cypresses and ginkgoes and podocarps spread out wide and there were dense beds of flowers, meadows of cinnamon ferns. If there were dinosaurs, we didn't see them. Maybe it was fog or the unrelenting rain but it was unnerving because there was a rich symphony of sounds. Some were the booming and braying of Hadrosaurs. We'd heard them during training. They were far distant. Others were close, the monkey chattering and argumentative songs of small animals engaged in the battle to survive. If conditions such as these were common, sound was probably the only way to attract a mate or pick a fight. I'm sure many were asking, 'How *you* doin'?' or saying 'Get the hell off my property.' But there was not a slither or a scurry to be seen, and at last my nerve began to fail. I took a long draw on the rebreather then waved Cassie, on point, back to me. We took a knee.

'I don't like this,' I whispered.

She pushed back the hood of her ghillie suit and ran a gloved hand through her bleached blonde, close-cut hair. It was strange seeing her without makeup.

'We got about another two miles to the hide. And it starts thinning out from here.'

She smiled and hefted her shotgun. 'We'll be fine.'

As is so often true in the politics of denial, her breezy confidence enabled me to ignore my nagging fears.

She was right though, and the forests thinned. This put us at the mercy of the rain and fog but we were at one with nature. I wanted to glory in it, not worry about drone coverage and the vague notion we perhaps should have listened to the sage advice of the FOB *patrons*.

The woods continued to thin but it was not an environmental shift; many of the trees and shrubs had been overturned, the trunks of the smallest sheared apart, their branches and twigs stripped. The fern meadows had been flattened into a thick duff of dung and fronds that no doubt added to the ageless mulch that carpeted the floor. There was dung everywhere, piles of it. It attracted birds and we saw our first dinosaur of the day, a moment I felt we should always mark.

It was a *Saurornitholestes*. The little bird lizard was a male, bedecked in iridescent plumage, his flightless wing-arms tucked tight against his lithe frame, its tail weighted down into a gentle arc by vanes arranged in such a way that the tail itself looked like one large feather. Rictal bristles fluttered on his eyelids and flowered around his snout.

To the untrained eye, he'd have looked like just another beautiful bird, but to me he was a natural wonder. The shame of it was that he was not doing something sublime like sunning himself or displaying for a mate, but rather he was rooting through shit. Still, he got what he came for. A quick scrabble in the dung and there came a sudden squeal, cut short, and then the little raptor was trotting off with a furry body with a long tail suspended in his jaws.

The damage to the forests worsened. It looked like the passing of a tornado or a hurricane. Were it not for the lack of ash, I'd have believed a pyroclastic cloud had blasted through this vicinity.

However, the cause of all this destruction was the foraging of *Einiosaurus*. A huge herd of them was nesting nearby and it was there our hide was hidden, overlooking the colony amongst the rough and rumble of shattered trees. But time was against the herd now; they needed tons of forage daily to support the young whose growth they needed desperately to fuel. The local woodlands were stripped clean, ruined but for the new growth already yielding green shoots to the sky. Every day, one parent or the other ran the gauntlet of predators ringing the colony in teeth and claws; every day they travelled further and further afield to bring back crops of pulp for the young and every day while the young grew fatter, the adults grew leaner and weaker. Every day, some would fall to the predators, some to exhaustion or injury, and every day a nest of hatchlings growing to calves would find them alone. Abandoned, they became prey for those predators bold enough to risk trampling or impalement by the increasingly cantankerous adult Einosaurs who stayed to protect the babies.

But the dead piled up. Illness took as many as predators, who often conducted mercy killings on the sickly adults while few of the young lived to suffer at the hands of starvation. Some adult Einosaurs came back sporting horrific injuries, slashing wounds on their thighs and flanks, semi-circular bites out of their tails. Stalwart and with a reptilian resignation they struggled on; some healed, the maggots cleaning out their wounds; some didn't, turned to living skeletons by bacteria or fungus.

The colony now looked like the remains of a Napoleonic battlefield, covered in adult bodies that looked like blasted fortifications, skeletons like wheel spokes, and bodies everywhere, while overhead, scavenging birds circled remorselessly. Our first day at the hide, we'd worn the rebreathers. It helped with the smell. It was the stench not just of rotten flesh but of rotten vegetation and rotten eggs. We had sat thunderstruck while trying not to puke when the wind shifted and blew the fug into the hide. Through binoculars we watched raptors, so beautiful as they went about their ugly business, wrestling baby Ceratopsians almost as large as they were out of their nests. The cries of the baby would sometimes bring an adult charging in but as it was invariably not their own nest, once the raptors had scattered it would leave and the hunters would return and continue on. These calves died slowly, the raptors lacking the killing power to put an end to the suffering with any speed. And usually one became two became three became more. These were not packs but mobs.

In the morning, at dusk and probably at night, racoon-sized mammals would dart out from amongst the treeline, such as it was, to grab any baby they could carry. They were already fat on egg yolk and embryo and all that protein had made them tough enough to take hatchlings. It was still a risk, mind, as Troodonts and raptors who came for Einosaur young would still instinctively chase down a mammal laden with a struggling baby. Sometimes they'd abandon the baby and make a run for it. Sometimes they'd even make it back to cover. Sometimes they didn't. I've never liked rats and watching one of the Troodonts, so elegant and nimble, and somehow looking scarily intelligent, pin one of the mammals and cut short its squealing always made me feel better inside.

But to me, perhaps the most terrifying of the predators

attending the colony were the varanids, the monitor lizards, some as big, if not bigger than many of the dinosaurs, implacable, seemingly invulnerable, with that shark-like rapacious patience. Their jaws hung with drool and wearing festering veils of flies, they would saunter in and take what they liked.

Of course, we also surmised the site would bring what we were there for: Tyrannosaurs, *Albertosaurus* and *Daspletosaurus*. We knew that adults of the latter, being habitual Ceratopsian killers, were present; sub-adults from both types were also there, drawn to the rich scents and apparently easy pickings of the colony. Similarly, it was very possible that adult Albertosaurs might also be lured at the prospect of tons of weakened Einosaur flesh, maybe hoping that chance would bring down an exhausted adult or risking a dash into the colony to snatch up some hapless babies.

So, this seemed like the perfect place to set up our hide. I could sit and sketch while Cassie would sit draped across her beloved Ruger and stare out at the nests, ranging her sights into the no-man's land around the colony and willing a magnificent Tyrannosaur to come striding from the shattered woods around us.

The stream wound on. Felled trees sometimes straddled it and we had to pick our way around them with extreme caution. We didn't want to trip or stumble any more than we wanted to walk into a juvenile Albertosaur.

The biggest pines and willows had been skinned of their bark. The Einosaurs had used their beaks to delicately shear it away. From the height of the damage some had even chanced walking up the trunk on their hands until they were standing upright as bears. From there, they had pruned away the higher branches and stripped off the bark. The air smelt of resin and compost.

Mist swarmed across the water. Rain made the stream's surface shimmer with ripples. Looking at the surrounding carnage it was hard to imagine how the flora would bounce back. But then you saw the dung and realized that the circle of life was death and defecation offered as fertilizer for the new saplings and sprouts fingering their way up through the battlefield detritus. Ferns and flowers would soon bedeck the woods once more.

In the meantime, there was still food enough if you knew where to look. Carrie raised a fist and I dropped to one knee, water gurgling around me.

She pointed. Up ahead was a Struthiomimid. It was a male, nervous, fidgeting and fussing in the stream's centre. He looked about constantly while his down rustled like a sack of shredded paper.

The reason for his concerns became clear when a female stepped out of the woods and strode anxiously out to join him. A second followed, at the head of a crèche of babies who bumbled along behind, little dust bunnies of fluffy down wetted into clusters of spikes so that they looked like sea urchins as much as baby dinosaurs. The females outstretched their wings and the chicks skittered into the shade they cast (which, under the miserable grey of the morning, wasn't much), hiding from the rain perhaps or feeling safer in the psychological protection they cast. The male led the flock across the stream until there were four females and innumerable chicks gathered around a fallen plane tree still rich enough with fruit. There were grape vines as well, and the adults picked off the fruits and fed them to the young.

Awww, I thought as I watched. So sweet. Then Cassie waved us on and we moved slowly. Adult ostrich dinosaurs could kick and their long-fingered hands could claw or grip you tightly when their taloned toes disembowelled you. And these ones had young so it was imperative that we move cautiously, our ghillie suits swallowed up in the forest and the fog.

We hadn't gone very far when Cassie turned back to me, but kept looking down the stream, into the haze. She once more waved me down onto a knee. I felt suddenly vulnerable and looked about. The trees, wounded, their crowns pruned, their trunks traumatized, crowded about me, all full of shadows, while the rain bore down and the fog swirled, and everything was out of focus.

Cassie started to back up, bent double, shotgun in her hand. She knelt and opened the breech to check what round she was loaded with. Then, she switched it out for another.

I frowned and my chest tightened.

'What is it?' I hissed, but she waved me off and just pointed ahead with the blade of her hand.

Up ahead, wood cracked and leaves rustled; then came a deep burbling – a big animal call. Out of the fog sloshed an Einosaur. Their eyesight wasn't great and if we kept still, chances were he wouldn't see us, although my real concern was that he'd take our ghillie suits for a tasty snack. We did our best to sink into the woods, getting lost amongst the boxwood and coral ferns.

The big Ceratopsian trudged up the stream towards us but paused to take a drink. He cupped water into the claw-shaped hollow at the pointed tip of his lower jaw and tilted back his massive head to let it trickle into his throat. He repeated this several times.

This was a big male, 15ft if he was an inch and a solid, truculent ton and a half. The huge forward-inclined horn bent far enough to touch the tip of his beak and was as battered and cracked as rough hewn wood; it looked more like it had been carved than grown. The warpaint of his frill was dull but still striking despite the gloom of the woods and he had scars on his flanks, one a long, deep grove of rugose tissue, perhaps from a rival's horn, or more likely from the slashing attack of a Tyrannosaur. I felt the compulsion to pull my pad but perhaps Cassie was psychic because she turned back and gave me a look that I felt even though her face was hidden by the ghillie suit.

Thirst slackened, he gave a sharp cough and came about like a battle cruiser and pushed into the woods. Maybe the call had been a summons because more Einosaurs appeared. Some drank but others set about the few trees still standing at the water's edge. They tore up a maple and splintered its trunk into kindling. White-coloured waterbirds sat on their backs or stalked about their feet, occasionally startled into the air by the raptors that were also part of the Einosaurs' entourage. The raptors seemed of little concern to the Parkosaurs who were there to scrabble for tubers and roots, and any fallen fruits or nuts that the Ceratopsians left in their wake. When a *Bambiraptor* did get too close, a male Parkosaur flushed his mane of quills, rattling them while he hissed at the raptor, who decided to seek breakfast elsewhere.

Finally, Cassie backed up to me, eyes always forward, until I stopped her with a hand in the small of her back. She leant across to me.

'Get a drone to see how busy the stream is,' she whispered into the comms.

'Magmatic, Magmatic, this is Raptor Red.' Saying it out loud made me realize what a stupid call sign that was. I called again and the comms clicked.

'Raptor Red, this is Magmatic.'

'Magmatic, you may have seen the Einosaurs we've got ahead of us. Can you vector a drone to check the stream as far as the hide and see what the traffic is like.'

Magmatic acknowledged and went off to check.

I leaned forward so my head was close to Cassie's. Over the plastic drumming of rain on the suit, I asked Cassie,

'What do we do if the way to the hide is blocked?'

Even I thought she was being a bit *laissez faire* when she shrugged and said, 'We go around them.'

Going around meant going into the woods and the closer to the colony we got meant the greater the risk of blundering into trouble.

'Really?' I said, too loud.

'Well I'm not going back to camp, not having come this far.'

On the sound files, you hear me exhale.

'OK.' Again with the politics of denial. Having my own concerns overturned by one so much more relaxed and confident.

The comms clicked.

'Raptor Red, this is Skyray.' The drone operator. 'We have the drone overhead of your position but the vis is only about 50 percent. We have been checking the IR cameras and there are a number of Einosaurs ahead of you, moving mainly north-west, across your axis of march.'

Axis of march? I thought this was a pleasant morning stroll.

'And, weather check, we reckon the rain won't let up today. Aerostat is showing a tropical storm front coming in off the KIS (*Cretaceous Inland Seaway, another name for the Western Interior Seaway*); it'll probably be blown out by the time it reaches the high plains phase line, but there'll still be plenty of rain. Fog is also unlikely to lift today.'

The right thing to do, with so much uncertainty ahead, would have been to turn about and go back to camp, seeing out the rain in relative safety while the fog lifted.

Instead, Carrie just nodded and stood to watch the Einosaurs bulldoze their way deeper into the woods.

Then, without a word, she crouched and began to slowly stalk forward.

All I could say was, 'Copy, Skyray,' and follow her.

The closeness to the nesting colony became inversely proportional to our mounting excitement. There were indeed Einosaurs but we had to wait while another Ceratopsian herd passed, a bachelor herd of Chasmosaurs. There were maybe a dozen, all verbose and noisy, cracking heads and flashing warpaint at one another. We kept very still during their passing but I did risk a sketch. It was just a few simple lines of graphite that really didn't capture the energy and majesty of these creatures, but there really was very little that could, beyond seeing them in the chain-mailed flesh.

When we got to the hide, we found we'd had a visit in the night. Rabbit-like droppings were piled in one corner. We cleared them out and remembered to secure the fasteners when we left.

The hide was set in the axis between two deadfalls, the trunks shrink-wrapped in creepers and vines, and was surrounded by dense shrub. It was on a fairly steep rise which would probably have made it difficult for an adult Einosaur to make it up the slope without sliding back down. As such it remained largely unbrowsed.

We went through the semblance of a routine, Cassie mounting the Ruger on a tripod and sighting the various points where we thought a Theropod might appear, while I checked in with the Magmatic and made breakfast.

Then, I set up my optic and took a sweep of the nest, marked any new bodies that might be worth sighting and generally took the lie of the land. With the rain maintaining its even strength, many of the adults in attendance were standing or sitting over their nests, presumably to keep the young from becoming wet and chilled. Less experienced or concerned parents were bearing the rain stoically while they sat beside their wards, who were bundled together.

There were the usual ne'er-do-wells and privateers present. Varanids, perhaps chilled by the rain, sluggishly picked over one nest just out from the hide. Two of them, one half as big as the other, which made it about 12ft long, tore apart something dead in a tug-of-war. In a rough arc beyond the nests sat a number of *Saurornitholestes* and Troodonts, apparently content with a bit of inter-species socializing in the rain. They dozed, feathers and down matted, drab and grubby. Several of the raptors sat flank to flank, necks crisscrossed.

The one up side to the weather was that it dampened down the stench and encouraged the return of our appetites. We ate crackers and pate and drank OJ. We forgot the rules about covering food, something we'd have done without thinking if we'd been at Yosemite. When the Pink Team crew chief came out to pick me up, he looked in the hide and just shook his head.

Rat-, possum- and racoon-sized mammals darted amongst the nests. One nest seethed with their furry bodies as they scavenged whatever was dead. Probably starved babies or a clutch killed by disease. Whatever the cause, it was rich pickings for the mammals and one would occasionally depart, belly so swollen it had to waddle away. A *Troodon* sat nearby. At first I thought it was asleep but then one sly eye eased open to regard the possum as it tumbled to cover.

The little dinosaur rose slowly, wings tight against its side as though making itself more streamlined. The possum was either reckless or addled with meat and got just that bit too close. The *Troodon* sprang forward and snapped the neck of the mammal with its jaws and another line of mammal evolution was snapped off at the roots. The *Troodon* tossed back its head and tried to get the possum down in one and failed. Instead, he dropped it and tore the animal in two between jaws and claws then swallowed it down in halves.

I drew and Cassie made observations. We checked in with the drones and looked for Theropod signs but there were none. It was early afternoon when the clouds thinned and we had a burst of sun that bought life to the colony. For the first time we saw young Einosaurs being a little more proactive. They began to brave the world beyond the bowl of their nests. Still clumsy, they showed an innate instinct to charge at anything that moved. We laughed when they gambolled after mammals and each other, adults looming over them like mountain ranges.

Their enjoyment of this brief sunny interlude was interrupted by a huffing cough we knew was a warning to the young, who quickly swarmed back to the nest.

And here was a first; a *Prenoceratops*, a distant pig-sized relative of the rhino-sized Einosaurs. It was trotting through the nest site, grimly determined, steering away from adult Einosaurs but eyes everywhere, the mohawk of quills that ran from its hips to the end of its deep tail slung casually to one side. Occasionally it would snap the tail like a pennant, usually at a varanid but seemingly at anything the fearless Neoceratopsian felt deserving of its wrath.

Finally it found a small varanid dragging half a carcass from a nest, meat that was clearly rotten and rank with maggots, but the *Prenoceratops* trotted over and with little due diligence, grabbed the body and departed, the varanid left nonplussed.

I was finishing off a sketch of the incident when Cassie announced she needed to pee. The usual SOP was to use one of the piddle packs given to us for just such an eventuality. They were clean and safe, but Cassie was shy and liked to pee outside away from my prying eyes but in what would have been the full glare of the drones and her own headcam – if she hadn't covered that up.

Because of that, the FOB handlers didn't really figure out what was happening at first. There was no sound and the darkness was assumed to be Cassie covering the lens.

How the drone missed the young *Daspletosaurus* remains a source of mystery and speculation. The drone operators hadn't been remiss. They had not been dozing or slacking off. But recounting the incident, and checking the coverage, and talking to the crews, it just seems to have been bad luck. One of the drones was roaming the nest sight, checking, somewhat ironically, the edge for Theropods. The other was in orbit above us. The woods were dense and we found footprints that showed the Daspletosaur had stalked the colony's border that night. It had been presumably sleeping in the dense woods above the hide at the summit of the slope, but in its lee; the ridge created by the rise created a blind shadow so the Theropod went unseen until it was too late.

Maybe it was the food. Maybe it was the acrid tang of Cassie's pee. Whatever it was that drew it to her, it caught her quite literally with her pants down. The shotgun was still on the ground where she'd left it.

The official report would read that the Theropod surprised her from behind. It's amazing how quietly even the biggest animals can move, especially in dense forest, barely cracking a twig. She probably never saw it coming. But in those long dark nights of the soul, I sometimes wonder if some instinct made her turn and she saw teeth-studded jaws bearing down on her. Maybe she threw up a hand in some desperate effort to ward off the attack. I even stood in a museum once and played it out with a cast of an *Albertosaurus*.

I didn't even realize how long she'd been gone, and if I had I'd have just assumed it was stomach trouble. Besides, I was busy drawing. The first I knew something was awry was the yelling on the comms, so loud I ripped the headset away.

That her torso was being downed by the young Daspletosaur never crossed my mind and when I stepped out of the hide, I just froze. My hand was resting on the shotgun and stayed there, even when the Theropod eyed me indifferently. Its head, its face, is indelibly written into my mind. The rain dripping from the end of its scaly, boiled leather snout. Cassie's legs hanging from its jaws. She'd lost a boot and her white sock was covered in blood. More blood cascading from the Daspletosaur's lips. The bristles of adult plumage pushing through, so much smoother and sleeker. The tiny arms tucked against the chest, hidden by long vanes so that only the two horrific claws protruded.

It never occurred to me to shoot it much less kill it. I just stupidly yelled 'shoo.'

Then, without a glance backwards it slipped back into the woods from whence it had come.

When the Pink Team arrived, I was sitting in the hide with Cassie's boot, which I'd found near where she'd been squatting. The crew chief packed my Bergen, including my sketchbook, but he took the boot from me. We tussled because it was all that was left of Cassie but it was technically MHC® property and would be part of their investigation.

Back at the FOB I never left my room until I returned home. I just couldn't bear the thought of the crewmen looking at me, thinking that I didn't have the Right Stuff. No one ever said it was my fault, and I know it was six of one and half a dozen of the other, but at the end of the day the only real judgement came from the Daspletosaur, whose indifference to me showed that indeed a stock portfolio counted for shit out there.

After a period of counselling, Nicci Holmes returned to a career at the Chicago stock exchange; she still hunts but restricts her activities to deer and wildfowl. She was recently quoted as saying, 'Every time I sight down my weapon, I'm seeing the eye of that Daspletosaur.'

HELL CREEK FORMATION

Period: Latest Cretaceous
Age: Maastrichtian stage (67–65 mya)
Present location: North America
Reserve size: 1,800 square miles

CONDITIONS

Located in what is now the Midwest of the USA, Hell Creek sits on the western side of the Western Interior Sea, by now little more than an epeiric arm of its former self. The North American continent was more or less in its current position even if the landmass exhibited various differences in shape. A continued downward trend in global temperatures led to the formation of polar icecaps that led to a worldwide drop in sea levels. The WIS as seen in the Campanian has reduced by some 40 per cent so that the interior sea is now just a finger of shallow inland seas and narrows that run roughly north–south from a polar sea.

This general cooling led to more pronounced winters to the north but Hell Creek remained relatively mild year round, with regular rainfall that kept the coastal regions lush and subtropical. Carbon dioxide levels continued to fall but were still double those of current levels (requiring the mandatory use of rebreathers).

GEOGRAPHY AND ENVIRONMENT

The Rockies continue to develop and shape the weather to the east. Hell Creek is beyond the range's rain shadow and receives rain pretty much year round. The weather stays balmy, rarely falling below 13°C (55°F) in the winter, and only below freezing under the most adverse of conditions. The topography is relatively level, the environment made up of what was the Interior Sea's bed.

Much of the reserve's western landscape is forest broken up by rivers, some of which are huge, flowing eastward. The rivers feed various tributaries and streams that in some places become soda lakes, the result of salt deposits from the retreating seaway.

The forests are dominated by angiosperms. Gallery forests of dawn redwood grow to hundreds of feet high; they are surrounded by dense stands of katsura, breadfruit, barberry, beech, plane trees, live oak and sycamore, palms and laurels; magnolias were also very common. Gymnosperms are also present, including *Araucarians*, conifers, cycads and podocarps. There are dense understoreys of many different species of fern and flowering shrubs and creeping vines. The forests thin in places to woodland and meadows of ferns and palmetto. The relatively benign climate means the trees do not shed their leaves or needles. However, after the season when daylight hours shorten and growth rates slow ('winter'), a growth season does occur.

Further east, the forests open up into flats of conifers, cypress domes and live oak, the trees scattered over fern and palmetto meadows. The rivers begin to branch more often and form deltas and peat swamps. These deltas give way to floodplains and coastal flats of sand and mud deposited by the rivers emptying into the shallow sea. Cypress domes are replaced by hundreds of small mangrove islands. These 'everglades' have a relatively modern appearance but they are far less widespread than in the Campanian, which could explain the disappearance of many of those Hadrosaurs and Ceratopsians that spent much of their time in the wetlands.

The rich landscape supports large numbers of dinosaurs; with feed available virtually all year round, many herbivores form localized populations of small herds. Others, such as *Edmontosaurus* and the northern *Triceratops*, are migratory, heading north to take advantage of the short growing season within subarctic regions. They head to the plains and woodlands that edge the polar sea; many nest there and bring their young back south in time for the 'spring' growing season.

LICENSED TARGETS

You are licensed to hunt the following species in Hell Creek:

TYRANNOSAURUS

Length: 40ft
Weight: 7 tons
While there are other carnivorous dinosaurs that claim to be bigger or longer, there can be none that are greater, and it is the thrill of hunting the ultimate dinosaur that makes Hell Creek the most popular of MHC®'s destinations.

We'll never know in what direction Tyrannosaur evolution was heading and as such *T-rex* remains the ultimate expression of these impressive predators. Its body plan is not too different from earlier Tyrannosaurs: the long tail counterweighting the huge head – in this case massive and thickset. Features alluded to in early forms became fully expressed in *T-rex*; the snout has narrowed to allow increased binocular vision. The teeth in the snout have kept their D-shaped cross-section while those behind are banana-shaped with an oval cross-section and serrations on both edges. They are larger in the upper jaw and operate along a 'knife and fork' principle, the smaller lower teeth pinching the flesh of the Tyrannosaur's prey up against the steak-knife upper teeth. The powerful S-curved neck can then draw the massive jaws backwards and the serrated teeth slice the flesh open like a huge scalpel blade.

T-rex hind legs are powerfully built; they are not as graceful as the likes of *Albertosaurus* but they are more than capable of supporting *T*-rex's heavier build whilst providing it with enough power for adults to out-pace the largest prey (and humans…). The forearms seem pathetically small but they are heavily muscled and sport large talons. They fulfil various functions; males use them to steady themselves during mating (along the lines of a Sauropod's spur) while females use them to manipulate eggs in the nest and cover and uncover the clutch, regulating its temperature (she will also use her snout and even her jaws for the same purposes). This is all done through touch.

This type of Tyrannosaur physiology applies to the adults. The young are very different; the fact is that the transition from juvenile to sexually mature adult is the most extreme of all the Tyrannosaurs. The mating season is generally at the end of 'winter' as the days lengthen and herald the new

A female *T-rex* has fought and bitten off the arm of a prospective mate after his mating overtures were rejected. The fighting has left her with a number of injuries.

growing season. In Hell Creek, where the population is largely localized (see below), males have established territories that usually overlap with at least one female. The male roars to attract the female; he will then court her.

This is a dangerous time for male Tyrannosaurs. Sexually dimorphic, the females are as much as a quarter larger than the males (who are generally recognizable by the more colourful plumage around their heads). If they do not find the male a suitable sexual partner, they are as likely to attack him as a competitor; males will also fight each other in territorial disputes, as well as competing for mates. Violence is only avoided if the roaring contest that precedes a fight sees one of the males back down. Females will also fight for similar reasons, including the right to mate with particular males.

As such, a *Tyrannosaurus* is far more likely to incur injuries from intra-species fighting than from prey.

Nesting occurs at the start of the growing season. Both parents attend to the eggs and hatchlings, the males keeping the female fed while she is brooding the 15–20 eggs. The babies grow quickly, fed by the parents until they are big enough to leave the nest. The young stay with their parents for some years – as many as five – not just to be fed (the juveniles are quite capable hunters almost from birth) but for protection. This is not just from adult Tyrannosaurs; these will take babies at any opportunity, but usually the young are too quick and small for fully grown giants; the main threat is from juvenile and sub-adult rexes (nicknamed by MHC® crews as princes and princesses).

These are the young that survived the first five years and are then abandoned by the parents. This sudden independence usually coincides with a sudden and continuous growth spurt that takes them to sexually immature adults over the next ten years or so. These princes and princesses are very different physically to the adults; they develop long, gracile legs and long jaws in narrow heads, and are quite capable runners.

They will often travel in bachelor packs of siblings although many live solitary existences; they fulfil the ecological role of mid-range predator that is often filled by completely unrelated types in other ecosystems. They are active, voracious hunters, preying largely on smaller dinosaurs, including hatchlings and juveniles, but mainly species that an adult would find hard to catch, such as the athletic Struthiomimids and Caenaganthids.

Reaching sexual maturity at about 20 years old, the adults increase in mass and strength, and develop into 'land sharks' – true ambush predators who now specialize in larger prey such as adult Edmontosaurs and *Triceratops*. As the most common animal in Hell Creek, the latter is a favoured food item, if much more dangerous than the former. This, of course, explains the shift to ambush predation.

These ambush tactics are not unlike those of the Campanian Tyrannosaurs; a charge from cover, possibly a short chase, and the delivering of a savage bite, usually to the flank or thighs. The wounded animal is then stalked and further bites inflicted if possible, until the prey is weak enough to be dispatched.

Older rexes are also frequent scavengers. The generally densely covered landscapes they inhabit means that smell is important in detecting prey both living and dead, but for the kill, stereoscopic vision allows the accurate delivery of the incapacitating bite.

There are both local and transient populations amongst Hell Creek's *T-rex* community. The transient population is usually made up of the more active sub-adult grouping, who travel with the herds of large dinosaurs, preying on younger animals, but even risking attacks on adults too sick or exhausted to fight back. On the way back south, they have the new crop of young to hunt.

TRICERATOPS

Length: 30ft
Weight: 8–10 tons
The most common of all Hell Creek dinosaurs is also one of the most famous, and if *T-rex* represents the ultimate in Tyrannosaur design, *Triceratops* is the epitome of horned dinosaur evolution. By the end of the Maastrichtian (and the Age of the Dinosaurs) the two species of *Triceratops*, *T. horridus* and *T. prorsus*, were filling all the ecological niches previously filled by a large number of types from the two Ceratopsian subfamilies. It is also the last known member of the Chasmosaurines (the only other known Ceratopsids to make it to the end of the Maastrichtian are the less common, more southerly *Torosaurus* and a species of *Pachyrhinosaurus* to the far north).

In terms of physiology, it is not too different from earlier Ceratopsids; its build is broadly similar; it features the same 'porcupine' spines on its rump and thighs and the stiff, quill-like mane running the more forward length of the tail, although they are slightly more pronounced in *Triceratops*. Both species also have the same powerful beak and shearing teeth batteries, and the same trio of two very long brow horns (in large individuals, these can be over 3ft long) and a smaller nasal horn.

Sexual dimorphism is limited to size and shield shape; the males are a little larger and have larger brow horns, while the frills of sexually mature females take an almost elongated heart shape (not dissimilar to *Torosaurus*, with which it can sometimes be confused in areas where their territories overlap, south of Hell Creek). The epoccipital hornlets outlining the fringe also tend to be larger in males.

Both horns and shield have defined proactive functions. At the start of the 'spring' breeding season, the male stakes out a territory and calls for females, which he then impresses with flashy visual displays on his shield and also the mane. The female can also signal her intentions with her shield, dull colours showing a lack of interest while bright ones can be taken as a 'come on' to her suitor. Males also fight for the best-positioned territories; these battles can take the form of more passive shows of force using the colours of their frills

A pair of male *Triceratops* prepares to charge one another in a duel over females.

and with vocalizations. However, should neither protagonist be willing to back down, fighting will take place; these battles can be quite prolonged and brutal; most adult males carry injuries to their face and shield, usually inflicted by their opponents' brow horns but sometimes including bite wounds from an attacker's beak. Some of these can be severe; puncture wounds, snapped horns left in the recipient of a charge, even lost eyes. Accordingly, the breeding season is something of a boom time for Tyrannosaurs; adult

Triceratops, usually difficult prey for even the fittest *T-rex*, are left exhausted by constant fighting. Others are weakened by injuries or blood loss. As such they make easy pickings for parent Tyrannosaurs with chicks to feed.

That said, a *T-rex* is happy to engage adult Trikes under almost any condition. This means that females are at just as much risk from attack, which is why dimorphism is limited to colours and shield – females are often required to fight for their lives and in these combats, size matters just as much to the females as the males. Both genders are also very aggressive, and it really pays to avoid getting too close. Their sense of smell is excellent, but their vision is also fair; however, not to the extent that it can differentiate a human from a young Tyrannosaur.

Trikes are also at risk as they do not run in herds; this is especially true of *T. horridus*, the more southerly of the two species. Living in a relatively benign climate, it is not really required to migrate as such and its populations are more localized. Its primary habitat is the lowland forests, woods and marshes, which are generally less conducive to socializing in large aggregations. However, they are common enough that random gatherings can inadvertently occur in areas where food is plentiful. These congregations can be fraught; females are generally intolerant of males outside of the breeding season and males can be overcome with machismo that leads to outbreaks of fighting.

Living a largely solitary existence that makes it vulnerable to predation may also explain *T.* horridus' belligerence. However, *T. prorsus* has a more northerly based habitat and is generally migratory. It heads north in large numbers at the end of the winter and breeds at the start of the spring growing season as the days lengthen.

Trikes nest colonially, both parents providing food for

the young only as long as it takes them to become precocial and leave the nest. In the case of *T. horridus*, the young generally scatter into dense forest until large enough to move out into open habitats, usually in small herds. In the case of *T. prorsus*, the infants then form a large aggregation that will travel with adults.

Triceratops also experiences broad ontogenic changes; as the horns and shield develop in the very young, the horns rise almost vertically and curve back, while the shield is similarly flattened against the neck. This is largely the result of being small, with threats usually coming from above. This state remains unchanged until sub-adulthood when the animal reaches a size to engage threats on a more or less horizontal plane. Then the horns begin to project forward and the shield rises up to present a more intimidating head-on view.

OTHER FAUNA

QUETZALCOATLUS

A member of the Azhdarchid family of giant pterosaurs, *Quetzalcoatlus* has a wingspan of around 35ft, presenting an incredible sight when airborne. However, you are more likely to see it on the ground, where it stands taller than a giraffe!

In essence, this great flier is a Tyrannosaur-sized stork or heron. Its long, stiff neck supports a massive beak somewhat akin to the likes of a very large saddlebill stork. On the ground it moves in a stilted fashion akin to that of a giant bat, on three robust fingers and toes. It can move with surprising speed at a stately gallop, but this is rare. It usually spends its time around watercourses, ponds and, when the ground is firm enough, marshlands. Carnivorous, its main prey is small vertebrates; the type of prey changes as the pterosaur grows. Sub-adults can fish and will take amphibians, small reptiles and mammals and even insects. The adults will generally take anything that can be swallowed down in one; this includes small and infant dinosaurs, the latter forming a major part of its diet during breeding season.

Populations of *Quetzalcoatlus* will also migrate north to hunt around the huge nesting colonies of *Edmontosaurus* and *Triceratops*. However, they are generalist predators and will take the young of *T. rex* and even small raptors. (They are quite capable of tackling humans – be warned!)

Quetzalcoatlus also frequents coastal regions, where it beachcombs and scavenges; it can often be seen following storms, scouting for any marine organism unfortunate enough to have been washed ashore. Scavenging forms a part of the pterosaur's diet and it will drive small predators from its kills.

The huge wingspan of *Quetzalcoatlus* makes it an excellent glider; it can travel thousands of miles and migrations run from north to south with some populations but also into the interior further west. Many nest around soda lakes and watercourses in the interior, while others fly up to the polar regions at the start of spring to make the most of the huge dinosaur migrations taking place.

Two or three eggs are usually laid in a scraped-out hollow in the ground; both parents attend to the young until they are old enough and big enough to fly. The young are vulnerable on the ground to attack from raptors and young Tyrannosaurs. However, they travel in small flocks for mutual protection. Adults are also social, staying together in mixed-gender groups – a single adult can fall victim to

Quetzalcoatlus **snaps up a snake disturbed by the grazing duckbill, *Edmontosaurus.***

sub-adult and fully grown Tyrannosaurs. However, these groups usually disband during the mating season, reforming only once the adults are free of their parental commitments.

EDMONTOSAURUS

The most common non-Ceratopsid larger dinosaur in Hell Creek, *Edmontosaurus* is a larger and very generalized Hadrosaur, large adults growing up to 40ft and weighing over 4 tons. As mentioned previously, the loss of wetland habitats at the very end of the Cretaceous resulted in the demise of many Hadrosaurs, especially the crested types; as such, the Maastrichtian duckbills are represented almost solely by this species. It is perhaps its generalist physiology and advanced feeding apparatus that allowed it to survive the environmental change, much as *Triceratops* did.

Equipped with powerful grinding batteries of teeth and a broad duckbill, it is generally a low-browser and grazer whose ecological role is very similar to modern herbivores such as zebra or bison. As such, its favoured habitat is open woodland, meadows and open prairie. However, it can also be found in marshlands, swamps and coastal wetlands.

It usually moves in small herds but at the end of winter, Edmontosaurs gather in vast herds that migrate northwards to nest in large colonial sites; the adults can then make the most of the spring growing season. The young grow fast and once they are big enough the herds reform and head south to spend summer on the fertile lowlands, where the aggregations scatter into smaller bands, often including young.

With Hell Creek being quite near, geologically speaking, to Dinosaur Park, there are a number of dinosaur types represented in both formations that are very similar to one another. These include:

Ankylosaurus; at 30ft long and weighing over 5 tons, *Ankylosaurus* lacks the more showy armour of the earlier *Euoplocephalus* but is much larger; it also sports a similar tail club. Generally solitary, it is relatively uncommon.

Pachycephalosaurus: The largest of the bone-headed dinosaurs who are named after it, *Pachycephalosaurus* is also the largest of its family, measuring over 15ft long and weighing nearly 1,000lbs. It is perhaps the most extreme version of the boneheads. The young are flat-headed but their pates are ringed in a crown of spikes and spines. The females keep this crown into adulthood but the males develop a massive bony dome. The microscopic construction of this helmet is, not surprisingly, unusual: it contains cells called fibroblasts; these generate collagen and extracellular matrix, the materials that form the foundation of cellular structures. Looking at male Pachycephalosaurs, this is hardly surprising. The dome is used in intra-species combat, predominantly at the start of the mating season. The males stand side-by-side and deliver powerful (and resounding) blows to their opponents' heads, necks and flanks. As a result many of the domes sport welts and lesions that the fibroblasts help heal quickly – an obviously vital attribute. It also means that the forest and woodland habitats of *Pachycephalosaurus* echo to the crack of heads in spring.

Anzu: A large Caenagnathid very similar to Dinosaur Park's *Chirostenotes* in most respects, including appearance and behaviour; it is, however, rather larger, at over 10ft long. It is also Hell Creek's most colourful inhabitant.

Acheroraptor: A small Dromaeosaurid raptor not unlike the more famous *Velociraptor* and quite closely related to it, it is quite rare in Hell Creek. It lives in the forests and open woodland as a solitary predator of small prey.

Leptoceratops: This large Leptoceratopsid (over 6ft long and weighing up to 400lbs) is a common sight in the woods and marshes of Hell Creek; unlike its Dinosaur Park predecessors, it is almost exclusively herbivorous but can be quite aggressive. Approach with caution.

Struthiomimus: Very similar in all aspects to the Dinosaur Park ostrich dinosaurs.

THE TRAIL

From Regicide: Hunting Tyrants in the Mesozoic *by Alessandra Vassileva; used with permission.*

Chance bent down and ungloved his hand. With his index finger he traced the outline of the footprint in the mud.

'15, maybe 20 years old... ' he murmured.

He wasn't referring to the print but the young *T-rex* who made it. He looked up and I followed his gaze down the river. It looked like the Prince – or Princess – was heading to the beach.

The comms chittered.

'Ahhh, Cromwell, this is Pink One Actual. You want us to task a drone to find the animal?'

Chance snorted. He didn't even bother looking up.

'Pink One Actual, that's a negative,' I said. 'We'll look for it the old fashioned way.'

'Copy that.'

'Print is pretty fresh,' said Chance.

I was watching the jungle that was rioting down to the river and swallowing up its banks. Thick boxwood and creeping ferns and bald cypress. *Glyptostrobus* knees rose out of the shallows, surrounded by duckweed. One of them was home to a trio of long-necked turtles and a Champsosaur, the four raised up in the morning light that filtered through the forest and fell on them as though they had been blessed from on high.

'How fresh is fresh?' I asked. 'Like, day old or hours?'

Watching the shadows, I never saw Chance shrug. Just heard the rustle of his ghillie suit. 'It's about half way between the high and low tide mark. Maybe three hours?'

'Okay,' was all I could think of to say. My crotch was itching and I wanted a change of underwear. The rebreather mask chafed. Sweat tickled the small of my back.

Something splashed in the river, something big. By the time I turned, there was nothing but ripples making the duckweed undulate. The river's edge was close. Danger close. Close enough for a croc to charge out of the water and grab Chance.

'Let's move.'

We followed the trail although sometimes that wasn't so easy. We picked our way through knee-deep mud and scouring rushes while a snow of catkin pollen swirled about us. Flies and biting insects bothered us, and we pulled down our insect hoods. We startled a flock of stilt-legged ducks that burst upward with the harsh breathing of flapping wings. Out of habit, I tracked them with the shotgun.

We struggled through moonwort and horsetails up onto a cypress dome. It was like stepping into a lung made of trees. The air was still and smelt of loam and flowers. Flowers were blooming amongst the serpentine twists of roots and branches, brightly coloured lilies and sundews. There were burrows in the mud banks beneath the mangle of roots.

'Probably crocs,' said Chance. He knelt in the rich earth. Ran a hand over it. 'No spores, no scat.'

Abandoned burrows then.

Golden light lanced in through the cypress canopies and made the dome a magical place and captured butterflies dancing. They were big, their wings the span of my hand. I watched entranced, but Chance knelt amongst the tracks of the Prince (we had at this point began to refer to the maker as a 'he'...). Leaving the end of the dome, he had waded the river. There was an obvious fording point that any experienced croc would know so we sat for a while glassing the water and the bank. But there were no nostrils flaring at the surface, no nictitating membranes unfurling from a golden eye. No log that might or might not be an armoured back.

Chance waded in while I covered him with the shotgun. He used a branch to gauge the water's depth but it never came higher than the top of his legs. But that was still deep enough to hide even a moderate-sized croc or a giant gar, and we didn't dally.

We were deep in the forest understorey now. It was a heaven of magnolia blossoms, great nimbus clouds of pink and white and others I didn't recognize that bloomed like cherry blossom and made the air and the ground white. Breadfruits and plane trees were laden with fruit, and the *Osmandia* ferns had ripened, turning the meadows gold. I pushed back my insect hood and pulled down the rebreather mask. The air smelt unbelievable. Like walking into a florists.

At the edge of a glade, Chance slowly raised a hand. It was a casual gesture, not the firm decisiveness of a hunter seeing prey. I stopped but didn't raise the shotgun.

He knelt and I followed suit. Looking back over his shoulder, he pointed ahead.

On the glade's western side, an *Anzu* was harvesting breadfruit. A male, it was a wondrous palette of colours, its parrot beak reddish-orange, its cassowary casque crimson and its face a deep yellow, from which its black eye stood out brightly. It had 'ears' behind the eyes, ovals of dark blue over white. Its throat was russet as was the leading edge of its flightless wings, while the feathered vanes they supported were a vivid vermillion but tipped in twilight blue. The underside of its neck and its belly were flaming white; the back of the neck was an iridescent purple and the back a shimmering blue, iridescent as well. Its pygostyle was bright purple, and the long feathers they supported an orangey-red tipped in white. Even the scales on its naked lower legs were colourful, the same colour as its beak.

I had never seen an ugly animal so beautifully coloured before. Its throat pouch was swollen with fruit which I suspected it was collecting for a nest full of chicks.

It was about as tall as Chance and had a kick like the proverbial mule so we really didn't want to disturb it, especially if it had chicks nearby. So, Chance looked back at me and with his hand swam around the glade in an arc.

I nodded and crouched low as we swung into the treeline, swallowed up in magnolia blossoms. We crept past the *Anzu*, which must have heard us because it suddenly froze then turned and vanished into the trees. You'd have thought an animal who moved in such beauty would have stood out like a sore thumb infected with luminous bacteria, but it didn't; it simply disappeared. The miracle of dazzle camouflage, I guess.

We picked up the Prince's trail, tripodal shapes in the duff of pine needles and dead leaves. It led us back down to the river. Here, the forest began to thin and give way to fern meadows, more golden *Osmandia*, bordered with chain ferns, cycads and *Onoclea,* broken by stands of palms and katsura with their gnarled grey bark. We stirred up a flock of Thescelosaurs (*a mid-sized Ornithopod*) who seemed to be uncomfortable with us, the weird shape of the ghillie suits not the familiar raptorial one of their regular predators but strange enough and mobile enough for concern. They watched us for a while then slowly returned to browsing, although one vigilant male stayed *en garde* until the river made a turn north and we disappeared from its sight.

In the crock of the oxbow that the turn created, the trees thickened into a small wood of *Araucarians*, sycamore and laurels, palm trees rising high amongst them. There was a sandy beach that followed the box in the river and on an upturned tree root we paused to take a drink and a bite to eat. We chewed on power bars and jerky, and enjoyed the sunshine while we watched waterbirds dabble for worms. On the other side of the river was a sea of reeds and what we took to be hummocks of earth or deadfalls amongst the softly swaying clatter of blade-like leaves. These rose out of the mud and manifested themselves into a small herd of *Triceratops*. We watched them through our optics. Covered in black mud that would soon dry to a cracked grey, it was hard to gauge their sex but it looked like a bachelor herd of young males.

This theory gained considerable weight when two of the Trikes began, for no discernable reason we could see, to have at it. They grunted and burbled at one another while their horns locked and wrestled, trying to twist each other over while circling about and kicking up geysers of mud and a cloud of waterbirds which had no doubt been enjoying their company up until that point.

It would be a stupid *T-rex* of any age that would try its luck with these recalcitrant young bucks so we moved on, hotly pursuing the Prince with all the speed we could muster, which was tough on foot in sweltering ghillie suits. I checked the time. We had about four hours before the Pink Team called bingo on us and we'd have to head back to the campsite. Or we'd have about three more than that before they would have to come in and pick us up then fly us back.

'Seven hours,' I reminded Chance.

'Ahuh,' was all he said, not looking back, just watching the prints left by the long stride of the Prince.

I wanted to remind him that night here came fast, but he didn't need reminding and wouldn't have cared anyway. That was my job: caring about the stuff that seemed trite but could get you killed. I asked Chance to hold up while I checked our position and comms checked with the Pink Team.

All was well and while he kept his irritation to himself, Chance gave me a look and then struck out once more on the hunt.

The fern meadows and reed beds gave way slowly to beach and the mudflats of the river's estuary. There were still cypress domes and palm stands but the landscape was far more open, and the Prince's trail became easy to follow. We squelched through brackish mud and tried to avoid stepping on the pink crabs that threatened us. A sea breeze came up, cool and strong enough to blow away the biting insects. The sand was white where it wasn't broken up by reeds and ferns.

Chance stopped dead. My first reaction was to shoulder the shotgun, but he just waved me forward. The smell of the sea gave way to something tangy and acrid. The Prince had taken a toilet break, leaving a pile of dung neat and tidy on the sand. A little raptor was picking its way through the droppings, looking for whatever it was it thought might be edible, I guess. It was strange seeing such a pretty animal doing such a noisome task. Toothed gulls, Icthyornids, gathered about it, looking for their chance.

We gave the dung a wide berth but, wow, that scat stank.

'It looked pretty solid,' said Chance. 'Pretty healthy individual.'

'No doubt,' was all the enthusiasm I could muster on that subject.

Finally, the flora thinned away to nothing but dried seaweed.

'Nice,' said Chance.

The beach was virgin white. It extended a quarter of mile eastward, flat, unbroken by dunes. The tide was out; we could see the greenish line that marked high water. Flocks of gulls stood out titanium white but for their red beaks against the sand. The sea beyond was a soft jade; the sky the definition of sky blue.

There was a temptation to throw off the ghillie suit, strip to our undies, call down the Pink Team and get a beach party going, but the moment passed when Chance set off remorselessly along the trail of fork-shaped prints.

Maybe another time, perhaps our last day in the Mesozoic. A chance to toast the demise of the dinosaurs.

I trotted off to catch up with Chance, checking about us. The wide open space of the beach meant we would easily see trouble coming but equally, trouble could just as easily see us. The ghillie suits were now plain silly against the crystal-clean sand and I was tempted to recommend we strip them off, but they were cool and who knew where the trail would take us.

As it was, it took us further down the beach. With the tide out, the beach gave way to old coral formations and rock. There were tidal pools and despite being in the Latest Cretaceous, I was tempted to go beachcombing. Others had the same idea. A lone female *Acheroraptor* (*a type of small Dromaeosaurid raptor*) was crunching down a small crab then turned to scrabbling around in the pools, looking for more seafood.

How sweet, I was thinking to myself, when the little raptor suddenly bolted and disappeared into white coral stone. Never a good sign. I shouldered my weapon and spun about, looking for trouble, but what I saw was a shadow undulating over the flats. I looked up and there it was: a *Quetzalcoatlus*, bigger than the drones, wings wider than the Victor orbiting overhead. It came soaring in low over the exposed rocks then flapped with a deep thud like a very distant explosion.

Further down the beach it wheeled and we had its vast wings in profile. Then they folded, and the giant pterosaur made a solid landing. It was at this point we realized there were two others on the ground already and the specks of white were no doubt gulls. It was also most definitely in the direct line the Prince had been heading.

Chance unshouldered his Ruger, took a knee, and removed the weapon from its case. Then he secured his shotgun across his chest. I could have tasked a drone to take a look, but where was the fun in that? Instead, we proceeded along the beach but at a more cautionary speed.

The pterosaurs and the attending gulls were having at something in the rocks. Maybe it was fish or shellfish, but the gulls suggested carrion of some ilk. Once we were closer, Chance said quietly and decisively, 'Glass it.'

I pulled out my optics and focused in on the scene. It was definitely something dead. I could see the tattered remains of a flipper. Some marine reptile had come to grief. The Quetzalcoatalids were picking their way carefully around the thing; one would occasionally bend its long neck downward and there would be a jerk of the head or a snap of the beak and then the great elongated bill would come up trailing red meat and the gulls would swarm in, and the noise would swell as they shrieked and cawed at one another, squabbling over the scraps.

But there was no *T-rex*. If the Prince had come this way he had since moved on. So, we stuck to the trail but not too closely, giving the pterosaurs a wide berth. However, it was not wide enough to miss the fact that the unfortunate centre of their charnel attentions was a turtle, the biggest I have ever seen. I mean, it was huge. Maybe there had been some event last night. The adults come ashore at high tide to lay their eggs in the sand and perhaps this one's timing was off. Either way, we could only surmise that it had been caught still ashore as the tide had started to go out. Heaving her massive bulk down the beach to the sea, for it almost certainly had to be a female, she had slipped into some crevice in the rocks that had toppled her onto her side. Hung up, unable to right herself, she was left there when the sun came up and her struggles drew the attention of the scavengers, including, perhaps, our darling Prince. Her back flipper was gone; there was nothing but a bloody hole that the pterosaurs were driving deeper and deeper into, while the fore flipper was bitten and ravaged.

Then, to my horror, I realized the turtle was still alive. Its beak was gasping, its eye wet and filled with that sad reptilian confusion and resignation of an animal quite literally out of its depth. This was of no concern to the pterosaurs, whose only concern was not stumbling themselves. The toothed gulls meanwhile hopped about the rocks and the carapace of the turtle, looking for the best spot to clean up. Some were even perched on the back of the pterosaurs, which moved with a strange grace on the ground; when one raised itself to its full height, it would have towered over an adult *T-rex*.

Now came the dilemma of the ethical, moral creatures that humans are. The turtle was being eaten very slowly alive. It was also being baked alive in its own shell by the sun. It was beyond saving but we were in a very strong position to put the animal out of its misery.

The ROEs strictly forbade us from interfering. Even so, Chance raised the rifle and sighted.

'Clean shot,' he said.

A *Quetzalcoatlus* drove its beak and tore away turtle. The poor creature's only mobile but half-eaten flipper waved pathetically.

The comms chimed.

'Ahh, Cromwell, this is Pink One Actual, what are your intentions?'

Chance chambered a round.

'Ahh Cromwell...?'

I glassed the turtle's face. It looked teary-eyed. I knew inside this was just to keep the eye moist but a softer heart could quite easily have believed the animal was crying. I imagined what the teams at the FOB were thinking while they watched our live feeds.

Pink One Actual came up again, firmer this time. 'Cromwell, may I remind you of the rules of engagement and penalty clauses in your contract regarding breaking the rules of engagement and the laws specifically relating to non-interference.'

'No, you may not. I am well aware of them. But I will remind you they were probably written by people who have never seen an animal being eaten alive.'

Unable to watch anymore, I turned away and headed back towards the trees where, fortunately, the trail led us.

Chance didn't follow at first. He had actually taken a knee and his eye was still on the Ruger's sight. His finger was on the trigger. Not on the trigger guard so there was no chance of a misfire. It was actually on the trigger. I saw his shoulders rise as he drew a breath. I sucked in one of my own. Would he...?

I wondered how long he could hold his breath. Wondered how long I could hold mine.

Then, his shoulders slumped as he exhaled. He lowered the rifle and stood.

I called his name and he sighed then turned. He looked at me and shrugged then we turned back for the trees.

I checked the time. An hour and a half until bingo. We were soon amongst the swaying beds of reeds and the floating heads of pollen and seeds. The sun was high but the sea breeze was pleasantly cool. Dragonflies bejewelled the long reeds and crocs basked on sand banks that we had to circumvent to get back on track. The trail wove back and forth along a winding channel that kept heading back to the beach then would reverse and back to the trees until at last we were amongst cypress domes and stands of palms, and spits of land covered in thick ferns.

And here there were Edmontosaurs.

The duckbills were browsing far and wide across the tidal flats, stripping ferns and browsing amongst the domes. The herd was large but strung out. There were crèches of calves learning the Hadrosaur menu from the adults they trailed. Although the young were old enough to feed themselves, an adult would occasionally half-eat a fruit-laden branch from a plane tree and leave the rest for the calves gathered about it. The yearlings were back with the fully grown as well, fit and healthy, fattening up on the fruits of the new season. They were even up for a little socializing, not quite sexually mature but willing to put in some practice, the bucks harassing the females, even the biggest adult ones, and getting brayed at and even bitten for their efforts. They had more success sparring with each other, shouldering and nipping at one another, slamming one another with their deep tails.

It was all very pastoral, but the Prince's trail led straight into the herd. We paused for a quick lunch and rehydration, while I checked our position. A salient of forest extended out from the main treeline, and it wasn't beyond the realms of possibility that that was where our quarry was heading.

I was making this sage observation to Chance when something disturbed the Hadrosaurs closest to us. There was a ripple of discontent and a swelling in noise. The adults had stopped feeding, and the calves had gathered into tightly formed crèches about them, sub-adults amongst them. One of the adults trumpeted out an alarm.

We turned to see where they were looking, at something further up the river.

And there she was. It may have been that our Prince was actually a Princess. We didn't care. We immediately moved in amongst the reeds for cover.

I glassed her. Chance was right – she must have been almost 20 years old. Maybe over a ton in weight and perhaps 8ft at the hips. She still had the long legs and jaws of youth, and was in her summer colours and plumage, and despite the alarm calls that were springing up around her, she moved with the elegance and casual swagger of an apex predator about to enter her prime.

That, of course, was nature's plan but, it was not ours.

The Edmontosaurs were moving further into the flats and away from the river, away from the Princess. Her course continued to take her towards us as she followed the river bank. The cypress was thick along the water's edge and she kept disappearing then reappearing a little further down the river. This made the duckbills even more agitated and there was a general movement by the herd away from the channel and deeper into the reeds and domes.

I checked in with the FOB.

'Potential target sighted.' It was a stupid thing to say; they knew this as well as I did but, you know, ROEs... 'Request permission to fire.'

There was a moment of consultation then the comms crackled. 'Permission granted.'

Chance pushed back his hood. He had his game face on, stoic and unemotional. He sighted down the channel.

Princess turned away from the river and began following the edge of the salient of forest, relaxed, it seemed, not really in hunting mode. She paused now and then to watch the Edmontosaurs retreat or sniff the air. She really was beautiful in that rough and ready frontier style. There were blackened scars in the down on her flanks that turned to white on the leathery skin of her belly. There were also puncture marks in her neck. Not a love bite but something altogether more aggressive.

The reeds made a prone shot impossible and kneeling improbable. Chance would have to take the shot standing.

I ranged the Princess. She was just under 150 yards out, to our north-west. The breeze was 4 knots, blowing westerly. Chance adjusted his sight and wrapped the rifle's strap about his shoulder then took his stance, feet firm against the earth.

He aimed.

The Princess had stopped and was perusing her domain.

Watching through the optic, I said softly, 'Ready when you are.'

It was quiet now. The Edmontosaurs had quietened and were feeding. Gulls cawed somewhere. The loudest sound was the breeze in the reeds, that sibilant rustle.

It was quiet enough for me to hear Chance draw breath.

The crack of the rifle was brutal. A split second after the report came the smell of cordite and, through the optics, dust exploded from the Princess. She staggered, and then I heard her roar in fear and pain.

But she didn't fall.

'Shit,' I heard Chance curse.

It was a wound. Not a kill. She looked about, frantic then disappeared into the forest.

'I was aiming for the head,' he said. 'I think I got her in the shoulder.'

I checked in with the Pink Team while Chance swore passionately beside me.

'Do you want us to finish her?' the gunship asked us.

Chance shook his head. Maybe there was too much pride at stake but I suspect we both couldn't take the thought of having someone else do the dirty work, no matter how dangerous it might seem.

'Cromwell, Pink One Actual. I would strongly recommend against going to those trees. At least let me task a drone with making an IR pass over them.'

'No,' said Chance. Pride goeth before a fall.

'We'll handle it,' I called. I tried to sound relaxed, but there was an edge in my voice when I said, 'But if you want to keep it tight over us, feel free.'

Even from here those woods looked awfully dark.

We slogged our way over to the treeline and scouted her last known position. There was blood sprayed over the trees. I wondered if she was presently drowning in her own blood. If the elephant load had struck her in the shoulder, it might have penetrated her lungs, which would now be filling up with fluid. I felt a pang of sympathy and the urge to finish her. She'd been too beautiful for a long, slow death.

But then again, she was wounded and the forest was deep.

We stood for a while in silence and listened. There was no panting or cries of pain. If we were lucky she would be dead already. But luck was a wounded Tyrannosaur today.

There came the clack of Chance cycling the Ruger. He studied the woods then turned to me.

'Drop the Bergen. We're going in light.'

I shrugged off the pack. All I would be taking was the shotgun, ammo, water and snacks.

'Looks like we'll still be putting something out of its misery today after all,' I snarled. Chance just gave me a look.

I informed the Pink Team of the plan, such as it was.

'Be careful,' came back on the comms.

'Oh, you can count on that,' I said, then Chance plunged into the shadows.

We hadn't gone far when we found more *T-rex* scat, voided, no doubt, in fear and pain. The blood trail was easy to follow and there were snapped branches; she had been staggering uncontrollable, trying to outrun the pain she was no doubt in, the panic that had no doubt seized her.

The magical stillness of the woods was replaced with a dark and solemn terror; this was the moment in the show where the two cops stumble into the serial killer's lair, where the fairy forest turns out to be full of monsters. I imagined a lot of eyes watching us from the shadows.

If Chance was feeling any of this, he didn't show it. He would stop occasionally and listen, or kneel and touch the ground.

We found Tyrannosaur vomit, semi-digested meat already swarming with flies and covered in the gouts of blood, the bits of lung that had been coughed up with it.

I kept hoping for a body but there was none.

We moved slowly and methodically. Chance would push a branch aside for me, and I would see the blood dripping from the leaves.

He stepped around tracks that grew fresher and fresher. The Princess was slowing, stumbling.

The comms chimed. I tapped Chance on the shoulder, and he took a knee.

The drone operator was an old hand. He spoke softly, kept his tone even.

'Cromwell, Hell Creek. Be advised. We got a paint on an

adult Tyrannosaur west of you, two klicks, coming your way.'

He was after the Princess.

'Cromwell, how copy?'

'I copy, Hell Creek.'

'Red One moving into overwatch.'

The gunship was orbiting the adult. I pulled the pad and called up the map display. Ahead the forest opened into a small glade bisected by a small stream. This, no doubt, would be the last resting place of our Princess, who was probably desperately thirsty with shock.

The surrounding woods were dense Bald Cypress and *Glyptostrobus*. Thick clusters of knees and roots running down to narrow mudflats. Gnarled stands of katsura. No place for an adult *rex*. It would have to come down the stream. On the image intensifier, I could see the Princess. Chance would be annoyed.

He wanted to do things the old fashioned way, but me, I didn't want to – ha ha – take chances.

'Cromwell, Hell Creek, are you moving?'

'Er, negative.'

'Copy, stand by.'

Chance looked back over his shoulder and frowned.

'Cromwell, we've got something at about your two o'clock position. Not big and moving slowly, but it's about 50 yards ahead of you.'

The forest bent in and breathed out more shadows. It was so quiet.

Chance cut in. 'Copy, Hell Creek,' he said softly. 'We'll confirm the target is dead then pull back to the river. You can pick us up from there.'

I shifted the shotgun. 'Are you sure that's a good idea? The gunship could finish her if she's still alive.'

Chance stood but didn't look back. 'I need to be certain.'

The emphasis was on 'I'.

I stood. 'I don't like it. That jungle is really dense and we don't know what's ahead of us.'

But Chance's ego was already buoying him forward. I was sweating into my ghillie suit when I followed.

The roots, the tangles of branches, katsura bark like shed snake skin covered in thick green mats of moss, hanging nooses of Spanish moss, scabrous fungi and rank mushroom farms – it all crowded in. The ground beneath was spongy with moonworts and liverworts. My boots squished into them and black water oozed up. Duckweed stuck to my toecaps.

Nothing big could hide here but it's what you don't see that kills you. Chance slowed. Up ahead, I could see a dappled light. Behind me, there was nothing but shadow.

He crouched now as he picked his way forward. Then he slowed and knelt behind a serpentine cluster of roots that was covered in vines. Purple grapes hung from them.

He waved me forward. When I knelt beside him, he gestured with his chin.

Amongst the clustered, clawed hands of cypress, the Princess had collapsed into the stream. At first I thought she was dead, but I glassed her and saw her flank suddenly heave as she struggled for a breath, the water rippling around her.

Chance lay the Ruger on a crux in the root.

I was watching her. Her eye was half open and a nictitating membrane drawn half across. She was half dead. Blood ran down the side of her jaw and from her nostrils, a seething scab of fly bodies. Her down was greasy and ruffled, not smooth and breeze-swept as when we'd first seen her.

I started at the rifle's report and the eye burst apart, the flies bursting into the air.

And that was that. The Princess settled like falling debris. Her tail gave a rattler twitch then uncoiled into the water.

I lowered the optics and turned to Chance. He had the rifle at port arms and sat contemplating the dead *rex*.

'Hate it when that happens,' he said.

I checked in with the Pink Team. Out target was dead but it felt messy, a Pyrrhic victory. She wasn't even an adult.

Chance was sloshing up the river toward the Princess when the Prince came.

He was probably no relation, was smaller than her, which is how he had been able to slip amongst the dense forest with ease. And he was covered in mud, which is why the drones had trouble picking him up. His heat signature was a scribble at best.

I don't think he intended to eat Chance; I suspect he was defending his new-found prize and Chance was about the size of a raptor or even a princeling in his eyes. Either way, he charged Chance, kicking up a fan of filthy water while I yelled a warning and unslung my shotgun. Everyone moved with a the grace of dancers.

I swung the weapon up to my shoulder and snapped off the safety in one seamless movement.

Chance effortlessly brought the Ruger up and cycled the weapon.

The Prince swung open his jaws and bore down on Chance with an athlete's poise and elegance.

That's how I remember it. I've never been able to watch the footage so I imagine it was a lot more running and screaming and panic. The Prince was about half as big again as Chance and despite his mass, moved with a predator's grace. His roar was like a volcano erupting in its mouth. It dwarfed the bark of Chance's shot, which went wide anyway. I wonder if Chance knew he could never get off a shot that would slow the Prince, let alone kill it, or if he just jerked the trigger on some primal instinct of self-preservation.

Those are just the things that haunt me at night.

Like it matters.

The Prince's maw engulfed Chance's head. The *rex* threw his long jaws back and forth, lifting Chance off his feet, sending water flying.

I fired. The slug hit the Prince at the base of the tail and he staggered, letting go of Chance with a metallic screech. He turned towards me, perhaps at the sound of the shotgun, and roared. I was looking down his throat about the same time I fired again and the shell blew out the back of the dinosaur's skull. His occipital condyle was splinters, his parietal calcium kindling. He dropped like the proverbial stone.

The only sound after that was the settling water and my own breathing. The smell of gunsmoke joined that of mud and rot.

As my mind and the smoke cleared, I finally caught up to the fact that Chance was no longer moving. I yelled his name and staggered over to where he lay. He was face down in the water but when I rolled him over, his head sort of stayed there, twisted at an impossible angle. There were great gouges in his chest.

I slumped into the water, only able to take solace in the fact that it was probably a quick death.

There were other sounds, mainly those over the comms. Lots of firm but understanding voices demanding sitreps. Was Chance dead? Yes, yes he was. Was the *T-rex* dead? Yes, very much so. His lifeless eyes were staring at me even as I spoke.

I needed to get out of there, apparently, because that adult *Tyrannosaurus*, attracted by all our noise, was making his way down the course of the stream.

In shock, I didn't really have the strength to lift Chance out of the water, but help arrived and the Victor's huge rotors shook the tree canopies overhead. I didn't have my Bergen so I didn't have the poncho I wanted to wrap him in but the crew chief, who had that look on his face of sad disappointment but complete lack of surprise, had one and we dragged Chance's body into it. Cocooned in plastic, he ascended from the forest and was pulled on board the tilt-rotor. I was next, lifted out on a jungle penetrator with the crew chief.

As we headed back, we passed over the *rex* who was about to have himself a square meal. All I could think was, *If only we'd taken the time to shoot that damn turtle…*

Alessandra has become an experienced scout and been back to the Mesozoic to hunt Tyrannosaurs on numerous occasions; such are her qualifications that she is a required travelling companion and scout for many hunters.

Now that you have completed this guide, please make your selections:

- ☐ CHINLE
- ☐ MORRISON
- ☐ BARAHIYA
- ☐ DINOSAUR PARK
- ☐ HELL CREEK

Once you have made your choices, please notify MHC® and await confirmation of your selection.

GOOD LUCK AND GOOD HUNTING!